The lifeguard, the same big blond one who'd attempted to rescue Dopey, sat up straight and suddenly lifted his binoculars to his face.

I, however, did not need binoculars to see what I saw next. And that was Michael finally breaking the surface after having been down nearly a minute. Only no sooner had he come up than he was pulled down again, and not by an undertow or riptide.

No, this I saw quite clearly: Michael was pulled down by a rope of seaweed that had somehow twined itself around his neck....

And then I saw there was no "somehow" about it. The seaweed was being held there by a pair of hands.

A pair of hands belonging to someone in the water beneath him.

Someone who had no need to surface for air. Because that someone was already dead.

Read Jenny Carroll's
The Mediator books:

Shadowland
Ninth Key
Reunion

And

1-800-Where-R-You books:

When Lightning Strikes
Code Name Cassandra

Visit Jenny at her Web site:

www.jennycarroll.com

The Mediator

Jenny Carroll

SIMON PULSE
New York London Toronto Sydney Singapore

First Simon Pulse edition June 2002

SIMON PULSE
An imprint of Simon & Schuster
Children's Publishing Division
1230 Avenue of the Americas
New York, NY 10020

Printed in the United States of America

10 9 8 7 6 5 4

ISBN 0-671-78812-4

In memory of J.V.C.

Reunion

CHAPTER

1

"Now this," Gina said, "is the life."

I was forced to agree with her. The two of us were stretched out in our bikinis, taking in the rays and balmy seventy-five-degree weather on Carmel Beach. It was March, but you wouldn't have known it by the way the sun was pouring down on us.

Well, this *was* California, after all.

"I mean it," Gina said. "I don't know how you do it every day."

I had my eyes closed. Visions of tall, icy Diet Cokes were dancing in my head. If only they had waiter service on the beach. It was the one thing missing, really. We'd already finished all of the sodas in our cooler, and it was a really long walk up the stairs from the beach to Jimmy's Quick Mart.

"Do what?" I murmured.

"Go to school," Gina said, "when you've got this fabulous beach just a mile or so away."

"It *is* hard," I admitted, my eyes still closed. "But

graduating from high school continues to be considered one of life's important achievements. I mean, I've heard that without a high school diploma, one doesn't have a hope of acquiring one of those high-powered service positions at Starbucks that I know I'll be angling for upon graduation."

"Seriously, Suze," Gina said. I felt her stir next to me, and opened my eyes. Gina had leaned up on her elbows, and was scanning the beach through her Ray Bans. "How can you *stand* it?"

How, indeed? It *was* gorgeous. The Pacific stretched out as far as the eye could see, turquoise blue darkening to navy the closer it got to the horizon. The waves were huge, crashing up against the yellow sand, tossing surfers and boogie boarders into the air as if they were pieces of driftwood. To our far right rose the green cliffs of Pebble Beach. To our left, the huge, seal-strewn boulders that were the stepping stones for what eventually turned into Big Sur, a particularly rugged section of the Pacific coastline.

And everywhere, the sun beat down, burning away the fog that earlier that day had threatened to ruin our plans. It was perfection. It was paradise.

If only I could have gotten someone to bring me a drink.

"Oh, my God." Gina tilted her Ray Bans and peered over the rims. "Check *this* out."

I followed her gaze through the tortoiseshell lenses of my Donna Karans. The lifeguard, who'd been sitting in his white tower a few yards away from our towels, suddenly leaped from his chair, his orange flotation device clutched in one hand. He landed with catlike grace in the sand, then suddenly took off toward the waves, his muscles rippling beneath his darkly tanned skin, his long blond hair flowing behind him.

Tourists fumbled for their cameras while sunbathers sat up for a better look. Gulls took off in startled flight, and beachcombers hurried to move out of the lifeguard's way. Then, with his lean, muscular body making a perfect arc in the air, he dove into the waves, only to come up yards away, swimming hard and fast for a kid who was caught in an undertow.

To my amusement, I saw that the kid was none other than Dopey, one of my stepbrothers, who'd accompanied us to the beach that afternoon. I recognized his voice instantly—once the lifeguard had pulled him back to the surface—as he vehemently cursed at his rescuer for attempting to save his life, and embarrassing him in front of his peers.

The lifeguard, to my delight, cursed right back at him.

Gina, who'd watched the drama unfold with rapt attention, said, lazily, "What a spaz."

Clearly, she had not recognized the victim. Gina had, much to my astonishment, informed me that I was incredibly lucky, because all my stepbrothers were so "cool." Even, apparently, Dopey.

Gina had never been particularly discriminating where boys were concerned.

Now she sighed, and leaned back against her towel.

"That," she said, shoving her sunglasses back into place, "was extremely disturbing. Except for the part when the hot lifeguard ran past us. That I enjoyed."

A few minutes later, the lifeguard came trudging

back in our direction, looking no less handsome in wet hair than he had in dry. He swung himself up to his tower, spoke briefly into his radio—probably putting out a B.O.L.O on Dopey: Be On the Look Out for an extremely stupid wrestler in a wetsuit, showing off for his stepsister's best friend from out of town—then returned to scanning the waves for other potential drowning victims.

"That's it," Gina declared suddenly. "I am in love. That lifeguard is the man I am going to marry."

See what I mean? Total lack of discrimination.

"You," I said disgustedly, "would marry any guy in a swimsuit."

"That's not true," Gina said. She pointed at a particularly hairy-backed tourist sitting in a Speedo a few yards away with his sunburned wife. "I do not, for instance, wish to marry him."

"Of course not. He's taken."

Gina rolled her eyes. "You're so weird. Come on, let's go get something to drink."

We climbed to our feet and found our shorts and sandals, then wriggled into them. Leaving our towels where they were, we picked our way across the hot sand toward the steep steps that led up to the parking lot where Sleepy had left the car.

"I want," Gina declared, when we'd reached the pavement, "a chocolate shake. Not one of those fancy gourmet ones they sell around here, either. I want a completely fake, chemically enhanced one, like they have at Mickey D's."

"Yeah, well," I said, trying to catch my breath. It was no joke, climbing up all those steps. And I'm in pretty good shape. I do a kick-boxing tape practically every night. "You're going to have to go into the next town for it because there aren't any fast food places around here."

Gina rolled her eyes. "What kind of hick town is this?" she complained in mock outrage. "No fast food, no traffic lights, no crime, no public transportation."

But she didn't mean it. Since her arrival from New York City the day before, Gina had been agog at my new life: envious of my bedroom's glorious ocean view, enraptured by my new stepfather's culinary abilities, and not in the least contemptuous of my stepbrothers' attempts to impress her. She hadn't once, as I'd expected her to, told either Sleepy or Dopey, both of whom seemed to be vying for her attentions, to get lost.

"Jesus, Simon," she'd said when I'd questioned her about it, "they're hotties. What do you expect me to do?"

Excuse me? My stepbrothers, hotties?

I think *not*.

Now, if it was hotties you wanted, you didn't have to look any further than the guy who manned the counter at Jimmy's, the little convenience store right across from the stairs to the beach. Dumb as an inflatable pool toy, Kurt—that was his name, I swear to God—was nevertheless stunning, and after I'd placed the sweating bottle of Diet Coke I'd secured from the refrigerated case on the counter in front of him, I gave him the old hairy eyeball. He was deeply absorbed in a copy of *Surf Digest*, so he didn't notice my leering gaze. I guess I was sun-drunk, or something, because I just kept standing there staring at

Kurt, but what I was really doing was thinking about someone else.

Someone whom I really shouldn't have been thinking about at all.

I guess that's why when Kelly Prescott said hi to me, I didn't even notice. It was like she wasn't even there.

Until she waved a hand in my face and went, "Hello, earth to Suze. Come in, Suze."

I tore my eyes off Kurt and found myself looking at Kelly, sophomore class president, radiant blonde, and fashion plate. She was in one of her dad's dress shirts, unbuttoned to reveal what she wore beneath it, which was an olive-green bikini made out of yarn. There were skin-colored inserts so you couldn't see her bare skin through the holes in the crochet.

Standing next to Kelly was Debbie Mancuso, my stepbrother Dopey's sometime girlfriend.

"Oh, my God," Kelly said. "I had no idea you were at the beach today, Suze. Where'd you put your towel?"

"By the lifeguard tower," I said.

"Oh, God," Kelly said. "Good spot. We're way over by the stairs."

Debbie went, way too casually, "I noticed the Rambler in the parking lot. Is Brad out on his board?"

Brad is what everyone but me calls my stepbrother Dopey.

"Yeah," Kelly said. "And Jake?"

Jake is the stepbrother I call Sleepy. For reasons unfathomable to me, Sleepy, who is in his senior year at the Mission Academy, and Dopey, a sophomore like me, are considered to be these great catches. Obviously, these girls have never seen my stepbrothers eat. It is truly a revolting sight.

"Yeah," I said. And since I knew what they were after, I added, "Why don't you two join us?"

"Cool," Kelly said. "That'd be gr—"

Gina appeared, and Kelly broke off mid-sentence.

Well, Gina is the kind of girl people break off mid-sentence to admire. She's nearly six feet tall, and the fact that she'd recently had her hair done into a mop of prickly-looking copper-colored tendrils, forming a four- or five-inch aura all the way around her head, only made her look taller. She also happened to have on a black vinyl bikini, over which she'd tugged on shorts that appeared to be made from the pull-tabs off of a lot of soda cans.

Oh, and the fact that she'd been out in the sun all day had darkened her normally café au lait skin to the color of espresso, always startling when combined with a nose ring and orange hair.

"Score," Gina said excitedly, as she thumped a six-pack down onto the counter next to my Diet Coke. "Yoo Hoo, dude. The perfect chemical compound."

"Um, Gina," I said, hoping she wasn't going to expect me to join her in consuming any of those bottles. "These are some friends of mine from school, Kelly Prescott and Debbie Mancuso. Kelly, Debbie, this is Gina Augustin, a friend of mine from New York."

Gina's eyes widened behind her Ray Bans. I think she was astonished by the fact that I had, since moving out here, actually made some friends, something I had certainly not had many of, besides her, back in

New York. Still, she managed to control her surprise and said, very politely, "How do you do?"

Debbie murmured, "Hi," but Kelly got straight to the point: "Where did you get those awesome shorts?"

It was while Gina was telling her that I first noticed the four kids in evening wear hanging out near the suntan lotion rack.

You might be wondering how I'd missed them before. Well, the truth of the matter is that, up until that particular moment, they hadn't been there.

And, then, suddenly, there they were.

Being from Brooklyn, I've seen far stranger things than four teenagers dressed in formal wear in a convenience mart on a Sunday afternoon at the beach. But since this wasn't New York, but California, the sight was a startling one. Even more startling was that these four were in the act of heisting a twelve-pack of beer.

I'm not kidding. A twelve-pack, right in broad daylight with them dressed to the nines, the girls with wrist corsages, even. Kurt's no rocket scientist, it's true, but surely they couldn't think he would simply let them walk out of there with this beer—particularly in prom wear.

Then I lifted up my Donna Karans in order to get a better look at them.

And that's when I realized it.

Kurt wasn't going to be carding these kids. No way.

Kurt couldn't see them.

Because they were dead.

CHAPTER 2

Yeah, all right. So I can see and talk to the dead. That's my "special" talent. You know, that "gift" we're all supposedly born with, the one that makes us unique from everyone else on the planet, but which so few of us actually ever discover.

I discovered mine at around the age of two, which was approximately when I met my first ghost.

See, my special gift is that I'm a mediator. I help guide the tortured souls of the newly dead to their afterlife destinations—wherever that happens to be—generally by cleaning up whatever messes they left behind when they croaked.

Some people might think this is really cool—you know, having the ability to talk to the dead. Allow me to assure you that it so isn't. First of all, with a few exceptions, the dead generally don't have anything all that interesting to say. And secondly, it's not like I can go around bragging about this unusual talent to my friends. Who'd believe me?

So, anyway, there we were at Jimmy's Quick Mart: me, Kurt, Gina, Kelly, Debbie, and the ghosts.

Whoopee.

You might be wondering why Kurt, Gina, Debbie, and Kelly didn't run screaming out of the store at this point. You know, seeing as how, on second glance, these kids were obviously ghouls. They were giving off that special *Look at me! I'm dead!* glow that only spooks have.

But of course Kurt, Gina, Debbie, and Kelly couldn't see these ghosts. Only I could.

Because I'm the mediator.

It's a crummy job, but somebody has to do it.

Only I have to tell you, at that particular moment, I wasn't too keen to.

This was because the ghosts were behaving in a particularly reprehensible manner. They were trying, as near as I could tell, to steal beer. Not a noble pursuit at any time, and, if you think about it, an especially stupid one if you happen to be dead. Don't get me wrong—ghosts do drink. In Jamaica, people traditionally leave glasses of coconut rum for Chango Macho, the *espiritu de la buena suerte.* And in Japan, fishermen leave sake out for the ghosts of their drowned brethren. And you can take my word for it, it isn't just evaporation that makes the level of liquid in those containers go down. Most ghosts enjoy a good drink, when they can get one.

No, what was stupid about what these ghosts were doing was the fact that they were obviously quite new at the whole being dead thing, and so they weren't real coordinated yet. It isn't easy for ghosts to lift things, even relatively light things. It takes a lot of practice. I've known ghosts who got really good at rattling chains and chucking books and even heavier stuff—usually at my head, but that's another story.

But for the most part, a twelve-pack of beer is way beyond your average new ghost's abilities, and these clowns were not about to pull it off. I would have told them so, but since I was the only one who could see them and the twelve-pack, which was hovering behind the lotion rack, just out of range of everybody else's vision but mine—it might have looked a little strange.

But they got the message without my saying anything. One of the girls—a blonde in an ice-blue sheath dress—hissed, "That one in the black is looking at us!"

One of the boys—they were both in tuxedos, both blond, both muscular; your basic interchangeable jock-type—went, "She is not. She's looking at the Bain de Soleil."

I pushed my DKs all the way to the top of my head so they could see that I really was glaring at them.

"Shit," the boys said at the same time. They dropped the pack of beer as if it had suddenly caught on fire. The sudden explosion of glass and beer caused everyone in the store—well, except for me, of course—to jump.

Kurt, behind the counter, looked up from his copy of *Surf Digest* and asked, "What the hell?"

Then Kurt did a very surprising thing. He reached under the counter and pulled out a baseball bat.

Gina observed this with great interest.

"You go, homey," she said to Kurt.

Kurt didn't seem to hear these words of encouragement. He ignored us, and strode over to where the pack of beer lay behind the lotion rack. He looked down at the foaming mess of broken glass and cardboard and asked, again, plaintively, "What the hell?"

Only this time, he didn't say *hell*, if you get my meaning.

Gina wandered over to look at the wreckage.

"Now, that's just a shame," she said, toeing one of the bigger shards with her platform sandal. "What do you think caused it? Earthquake?"

When my stepfather, driving Gina back to our house from the airport, had asked her what she most hoped to experience while in California, Gina had replied without hesitation, "The big one." Earthquakes were the one thing we didn't get a lot of back in New York.

"There wasn't no quake," Kurt said. "And these beers are from the fridge against that wall back there. How'd they get all the way up here?" he wanted to know.

Kelly and Debbie joined Gina and Kurt in surveying the damage and wondering at its cause. Only I hung back. I could, I suppose, have offered an explanation, but I didn't think anyone was going to believe me—not if I told the truth, anyway. Well, Gina probably would have. She knew a little bit—more than anybody else I knew, with the exception, maybe, of my youngest stepbrother, Doc, and Father Dom—about the mediator thing.

Still, what she knew wasn't much. I've always

sort of kept my business to myself. It simplifies things, you know.

I figured it would be wisest if I just stayed out of the whole thing. I opened my soda and took a deep swallow. Ah. Potassium benzoate. It always hits the spot.

It was only then, my attention wandering, that I noticed the headline on the front of the local paper. *Four Dead,* it proclaimed, *in Midnight Plunge.*

"Maybe," Kelly was saying, "somebody took it out and was gonna buy it, and at the last minute, changed their mind, and left it on the shelf right there—"

"Yeah," Gina interrupted enthusiastically. "And then an earthquake shook it off!"

"There wasn't no earthquake," Kurt said. Only he didn't sound as sure as before. "Was there?"

"I kind of felt something," Debbie said.

Kelly said, "Yeah, I think I did, too."

"Just for a minute there," Debbie said.

"Yeah," Kelly said.

"Damn!" Gina put her hands on her hips. "Are you telling me there was an actual earthquake just now, and *I missed it?*"

I took a copy of the paper off of the pile and unfolded it.

> Four seniors from Robert Louis Stevenson High School were tragically killed in a car accident last night as they were returning home from a spring formal. Felicia Bruce, 17; Mark Pulsford, 18; Josh Saunders, 18; and Carrie Whitman, 18, were declared dead at the scene

> after a head-on collision along a treacherous stretch of California Highway 1 caused their vehicle to to careen past a protective guardrail and into the sea below.

"What'd it feel like?" Gina demanded. "So I'll know if there's another one."

"Well," Kelly said. "This wasn't a very big one. It was just...well, if you've been through enough of them, you can just sort of tell, you know? It's like a feeling you get, on the back of your neck. The hair there kind of raises up."

"Yeah," Debbie said. "That's just how I felt. Not so much that the ground was moving *underneath* me, but like a cold breeze moved *through* me real fast."

"Exactly," Kelly said.

> A thick fog, which rolled in from the sea after midnight last night, causing poor visibility and dangerous driving conditions along the area of the coastline known as Big Sur, is said to have contributed to the accident.

"That doesn't sound like any earthquake I've ever heard of," Gina declared, the skepticism in her voice plainly evident. "That sounds more like a ghost story."

"But it's true," Kelly said. "Sometimes we get tremors that are so little, you can't really feel them. They're very localized. For instance, two months ago there was a quake that brought down a sizeable portion of a breezeway at our school. And that was it. No other damage was reported anywhere else."

Gina looked unimpressed. She didn't know what I did, which was that that chunk of the school's roof had caved in not because of any earthquake, but because of a supernatural occurrence brought about during an altercation between me and a recalcitrant ghost.

"My dog always knows when there's going to be a quake," Debbie said. "She won't come out from under the pool table."

"Was she under the pool table this morning?" Gina wanted to know.

"Well," Debbie said. "No. . . ."

> The driver of the other vehicle, a minor whose name has not been made available by the police, was injured in the accident, but was treated and released from Carmel Hospital. It is unknown at this time whether alcohol played a part in the accident, but police say they will be investigating the matter.

"Look," Gina said. She bent down and picked something up from the wreckage at her feet. "A sole survivor."

She held up a lone bottle of Bud.

"Well," Kurt said, taking the bottle from her. "That's something, I guess."

The bell above the door to Jimmy's tinkled, and suddenly my two stepbrothers, followed by two of their surfer friends, streamed in. They'd changed out of their wetsuits and abandoned their boards somewhere. Apparently, they were taking a beef jerky break, since it was toward the canisters of these, sitting on the counter, that they headed upon entering.

"Hi, Brad," Debbie said in this very flirty voice.

Dopey broke away from the beef jerky long enough to say hi back in an extremely awkward manner—awkward because even though it was Debbie that Dopey was semi-seeing, it was Kelly he really liked.

What was worse, though, was that since Gina's arrival, he'd been flirting with her outrageously, too.

"Hi, Brad," Gina said. Her voice wasn't flirty at all. Gina never flirted. She was very straightforward with boys. It was for this reason that she had not been without a date on a Saturday night since the seventh grade. "Hi, Jake."

Sleepy, his mouth full of beef jerky, turned around and blinked at her. I used to think Sleepy had a drug problem, but then I found out that that's how he always looks.

"Hey," Sleepy said. He swallowed, and then did an extraordinary thing—well, for Sleepy, anyway.

He smiled.

This was really too much. I'd lived with these guys for almost two months, now—ever since my mom married their dad, and moved me all the way across the country so that we could all live together and be One Big Happy Family—and during that time, I'd seen Sleepy smile maybe twice. And now here he was drooling all over my best friend.

It was sick, I tell you. Sick!

"So," Sleepy said. "You girls goin' back down? To the water, I mean?"

"Well," Kelly said, slowly. "I guess that depends—"

Gina cut to the chase.

"What are you guys doing?" she asked.

"Goin' back down for about another hour," Sleepy replied. "Then we're gonna stop and get some 'za. You in?"

"I could deal," Gina said. She looked at me questioningly. "Simon?"

I followed the direction of her gaze, and saw she'd noticed the newspaper in my hands. I hastily put it back.

"Sure," I said. "Whatever."

I figured I'd better eat while I still could. I had a feeling I was going to be pretty busy soon.

CHAPTER 3

"Ah," Father Dominic said. "The RLS Angels."

I didn't even glance at him. I was slumped in one of the chairs he keeps in front of his desk, playing with a Gameboy one of the teachers had confiscated from a student, and which had eventually found its way into the bottom drawer of the principal's desk. I was going to keep Father Dom's bottom desk drawer in mind when Christmas rolled around. I had a good idea where Sleepy and Dopey's presents were going to come from.

"Angels?" I grunted, and not just because I was losing badly at Tetris. "There wasn't anything too angelic about them, if you ask me."

"They were very attractive young people, from what I understand." Father Dom started shifting around the piles of paper he had all over his desk. "Class leaders. Very bright young things. I believe it was their principal who dubbed them the RLS Angels in his statement to the press concerning the tragedy."

"Huh." I tried to angle an oddly shaped object into the small space allotted for it. "Angels who were trying to lift a twelve-pack of Bud."

"Here." Father Dom found a copy of the paper I'd looked at the day before, only he, unlike me, had taken the trouble to open it. He turned to the obituaries where there were photos of the deceased. "Take a look and see if they are the young people you saw."

I passed him the Gameboy. "Finish this game for me," I said, taking the paper from him.

Father Dominic looked down at the Gameboy in dismay. "Oh, my," he said. "I'm afraid I don't—"

"Just rotate the shapes to make them fit in the spaces at the bottom. The more rows you complete, the better."

"Oh," Father Dominic said. The Gameboy binged and bonged as he frantically pushed buttons. "Oh, dear. Anything more complicated than computer solitaire, and I'm afraid—"

His voice trailed off as he became absorbed in the game. Even though I was supposed to be reading the paper, I looked at him instead.

He's a sweet old guy, Father Dominic. He's usually mad at me, of course, but that doesn't mean I don't like him. I was, in fact, growing surprisingly attached to him. I'd found that I couldn't wait, for instance, to come rushing in and tell him all about those kids I'd seen at the Quick Mart. I guess that's because, after sixteen years of not being able to tell anybody about my "special" ability, I finally had someone to unload on, Father Dom having that same "special" ability—something I'd discovered my first day at the Junipero Serra Mission Academy.

Father Dominic, however, is a way better mediator than I am. Well, maybe not better. But different, certainly. See, he really feels that ghosts are best handled with gentle guidance and earnest advice—same as the living. I'm more in favor of a sort of get-to-the-point approach that tends to involve my fists.

Well, sometimes these dead folks just won't *listen*.

Not all of them, of course. Some of them are extremely good listeners. Like the one who lives in my bedroom, for instance.

But lately, I've been doing my best not to think about him any more than I have to.

I turned my attention to the paper Father Dom had passed me. Yep, there they were, the RLS Angels. The same kids I'd seen the day before in Jimmy's, only in their school photos they weren't dressed in their formal wear.

Father Dom was right. They were attractive. And bright. And leaders. Felicia, the youngest, had been head of the varsity cheerleading team. Mark Pulsford had been captain of the football team. Josh Saunders had been senior class president. Carrie Whitman had been last season's homecoming queen—not exactly a leadership position, but one that was elected democratically enough. Four bright, attractive kids, all dead as doornails.

And up, I happened to know, to no good.

The obituaries were sad and all, but I hadn't known these people. They attended Robert Louis

Stevenson High School, our school's bitterest rival. The Junipero Serra Mission Academy, which my stepbrothers and I attend, and of which Father Dom is principal, is always getting its academic and athletic butt kicked by RLS. And while I don't possess much school spirit, I've always had a thing for underdogs—which the Mission Academy, in comparison with RLS, clearly is.

So I wasn't about to get all choked up about the loss of a few RLS students. Especially not knowing what I knew.

Not that I knew so much. In fact, I didn't really know anything at all. But the night before, after coming home from "'za" with Sleepy and Dopey, Gina had succumbed to jet lag—we're three hours behind New York, so around nine o'clock, she more or less passed out on the daybed my mother had purchased for her to sleep on in my room during her stay.

I didn't exactly mind. The sun had pretty much wiped me out, so I was perfectly content to sit on my own bed, across the room from hers, and do the geometry homework I'd assured my mother I'd finished well before Gina's arrival.

It was around this time that Jesse suddenly materialized next to my bed.

"Shhh," I said to him when he started to speak, and pointed toward Gina. I'd explained to him, well in advance of her arrival, that Gina was coming all the way from New York to stay for a week, and that I'd appreciate it if he laid low during her visit.

It's not exactly a joke, having to share your room

with its previous tenant—the *ghost* of its previous tenant, I should say, since Jesse has been dead for a century and a half or so.

On the one hand, I can totally see Jesse's side of it. It isn't his fault someone murdered him—at least, that's how I suspect he died. He—understandably, I guess—isn't too anxious to talk about it.

And I guess it also isn't his fault that, after death, instead of going off to heaven, or hell, or on to another life, or wherever it is people go after they die, he ended up sticking around in the room in which he was killed. Because in spite of what you might think, most people do not end up as ghosts. God forbid. If that were true, my social life would be so over...not that it's so great to begin with. The only people who end up being ghosts are the ones who've left behind some kind of unfinished business.

I have no idea what business it is that Jesse left unfinished—and the truth is, I'm not so sure he knows, either. But it doesn't seem fair that if I'm destined to share my bedroom with the ghost of a dead guy, the dead guy has to be so cute.

I mean it. Jesse is way too good looking for my peace of mind. I may be a mediator, but I'm still human, for crying out loud.

But anyway, there he was, after I'd told him very politely not to come around for a while, looking all manly and hot and everything in the nineteenth-century outlaw outfit he always wears. You know the kind: with those tight black pants and the white shirt open down to *there*...

"When is she leaving?" Jesse wanted to know,

bringing my attention away from the place where his shirt opened, revealing an extremely muscular set of abs, up to his face—which, I probably don't have to point out, is totally perfect, except for this small white scar in one of his dark eyebrows.

He didn't bother whispering. Gina couldn't hear him.

"I told you," I said. I, on the other hand, had to whisper since there was every likelihood I might be overheard. "Next Sunday."

"That long?"

Jesse looked irritated. I would like to say that he looked irritated because he considered every moment I spent with Gina a moment stolen from him, and deeply resented her because of that.

But to be honest, I highly doubt that was the case. I'm pretty sure Jesse likes me, and everything. . . .

But only as a friend. Not in any special kind of way. Why should he? He's one hundred and fifty years old—a hundred and seventy if you count the fact that he'd been twenty or so when he died. What could a guy who'd lived through a hundred and seventy years of stuff possibly see in a sixteen-year-old high school sophomore who's never had a boyfriend and can't even pass her driving exam?

Not a whole heck of a lot.

Let's face it, I knew perfectly well why Jesse wanted Gina gone.

Because of Spike.

Spike is our cat. I say "our" cat, because even though ordinarily animals can't stand ghosts, Spike has developed this strange affinity for Jesse. His affection for Jesse balances out, in a way, his total lack of regard for me, even though I'm the one who feeds him, and cleans out his litter box, and, oh, yes, rescued him from a life of squalor on the mean streets of Carmel.

Does the stupid thing show me one iota of gratitude? No way. But Jesse, he adores. In fact, Spike spends most of his time outdoors, and only bothers coming around whenever he senses Jesse might have materialized.

Like now, for instance. I heard a familiar thump on the porch roof—Spike landing there from the pine tree he always climbs to reach it—and then the big orange nightmare was scrambling through the window I'd left open for him, mewing piteously, like he hadn't been fed in ages.

When Jesse saw Spike, he went over to him and started scratching him under the ears, causing the cat to purr so loudly I thought he might wake Gina up.

"Look," I said. "It's just for a week. Spike will survive."

Jesse looked up at me with an expression that seemed to suggest that he thought I'd slipped down a few notches on the IQ scale.

"It's not Spike I'm worried about," he said.

This only served to confuse me. I knew it couldn't be *me* Jesse was worrying about. I mean, I guess I'd gotten into a few scrapes since I'd met him—scrapes that, more often than not, Jesse'd had to bail me out of. But nothing was going on just then. Well, aside from the four dead kids I'd seen that afternoon in Jimmy's.

"Yeah?" I watched as Spike threw his head back in obvious ecstasy as Jesse scratched him underneath the chin. "What is it, then? Gina's very cool, you know. Even if she found out about you, I doubt she'd run screaming from the room, or anything. She'd probably just want to borrow your shirt sometime, or something."

Jesse glanced over at my houseguest. All you could really see of Gina was a couple of lumps beneath the comforter, and a lot of bright copper curls spread out across the pillows beneath her head.

"I'm certain that she's very...cool," Jesse said, a little hesitantly. Sometimes my twenty-first-century vernacular throws him. But that's okay. His frequent employment of Spanish, of which I don't speak a word, throws me. "It's just that something's happened—"

This perked me right up. He looked pretty serious about it, too. Like maybe what had happened was that he'd finally realized that I was the perfect woman for him, and that all this time he'd been fighting an overwhelming attraction for me, and that he'd finally had to give up the fight in the light of my incredible irresistibility.

But then he had to go and say, "I've been hearing some things."

I sank back against my pillows, disappointed.

"Oh," I said. "So you've sensed a disturbance in the Force, have you, Luke?"

Jesse knit his eyebrows in bewilderment. He had no idea, of course, what I was talking about. My rare flashes of wit are, for the most part, sadly wasted on him. It's really no wonder he isn't even the tiniest bit in love with me.

I sighed and said, "So you heard something on the ghost grapevine. What?"

Jesse often picked up on things that were happening on what I like to call the spectral plane, things that often don't have anything to do with him, but which usually end up involving me, most often in a highly life-threatening—or at least horribly messy—way. The last time he'd "heard some things," I'd ended up nearly being killed by a psychotic real estate developer.

So I guess you can see why my heart doesn't exactly go pitter-pat whenever Jesse mentions he's heard something.

"There are some newcomers," he said, as he continued to pet Spike. "Young ones."

I raised my eyebrows, remembering the kids in the prom wear at Jimmy's. "Yes?"

"They're looking for something," Jesse said.

"Yeah," I said. "I know. Beer."

Jesse shook his head. He had a sort of distant expression on his face, and he wasn't looking at me, but sort of past me, as if there were something very far away just beyond my right shoulder.

"No," he said. "Not beer. They're looking for someone. And they're angry." His dark eyes came sharply into focus and bored into my face. "They're very angry, Susannah."

His gaze was so intense, I had to drop my own. Jesse's eyes are such a deep brown, a lot of the time I can't tell where his pupils end and irises begin. It's a little unnerving. Almost as unnerving as the way he always calls me by my full name, Susannah. No one except Father Dominic ever calls me that.

"Angry?" I looked down at my geometry book. The kids I saw hadn't looked a bit angry. Scared, maybe, after they'd realized I could see them. But not angry. He must, I thought, have been talking about someone else.

"Well," I said. "Okay. I'll keep my eyes open. Thanks."

Jesse looked like he'd wanted to say more, but all of a sudden, Gina rolled over, lifted up her head, and squinted in my direction.

"Suze?" she said sleepily. "Who you talking to?"

I said, "Nobody." I hoped she couldn't read the guilt in my expression. I hate lying to her. She is, after all, my best friend. "Why?"

Gina hoisted herself up onto her elbows and gaped at Spike. "So that's the famous Spike I've been hearing so much about from your brothers? Damn, he *is* ugly."

Jesse, who'd stayed where he was, looked defensive. Spike was his baby, and you just don't go around calling Jesse's baby ugly.

"He's not so bad," I said, hoping Gina would get the message and shut up.

"Are you on crack?" Gina wanted to know. "Simon, the thing's only got one ear."

Suddenly, the large, gilt-framed mirror above the dressing table started to shake. It had a tendency to do this whenever Jesse got annoyed—really annoyed.

Gina, not knowing this, stared at the mirror with growing excitement. "Hey!" she cried. "All right! Another one!"

She meant an earthquake, of course, but this, like the one before, was no earthquake. It was just Jesse letting off steam.

Then the next thing I knew, a bottle of fingernail polish Gina had left on the dressing table went flying, and, defying all gravitational law, landed upside down in the suitcase she had placed on the floor at the end of the daybed, around seven or eight feet away.

I probably don't need to add that the bottle of polish—it was emerald green—was uncapped. And that it ended up on top of the clothes Gina hadn't unpacked yet.

Gina let out a terrific shriek, threw back the comforter, and dove to the floor, trying to salvage what she could. I, meanwhile, threw Jesse a very dirty look.

But all he said was, "Don't look at me like that, Susannah. You heard what she said about him." He sounded wounded. "She called him ugly."

I growled, "*I* say he's ugly all the time, and you don't ever do that to *me.*"

He lifted the eyebrow with the scar in it, and then said, "Well, it's different when you say it."

And then, as if he couldn't stand it a minute longer, Jesse abruptly disappeared, leaving a very disgruntled-looking Spike—and a confused Gina—behind.

"I don't understand this," Gina said as she held up a one-piece leopard print bathing suit that was now hopelessly stained. "I don't understand how that happened. First the beer, in that store today, and now this. I tell you, California is *weird.*"

Reflecting on all this in Father Dominic's office the next morning, I supposed I could see how Gina must have felt. I mean, it probably seemed to her like things had gone flying around an awful lot lately. The common denominator, which Gina still hadn't noticed, was that they only went flying around when *I* was present.

I had a feeling that, if she stuck it out for the whole week, she'd catch on. And fast.

Father Dominic was engrossed in the Gameboy I'd given him. I put down the obituary page and said, "Father Dom."

His fingers flew frantically over the buttons that manipulated the game pieces. "One minute, please, Susannah," he said.

"Uh, Father Dom?" I waved the paper in his general direction. "This is them. The kids I saw yesterday."

"Um-hmmm," Father Dominic said. The Gameboy beeped.

"So, I guess we should keep an eye out for them. Jesse told me—" Father Dominic knew about Jesse, although their relationship was not, shall we say, the closest: Father D had a real big problem with the fact that there was, basically, a boy living in my bedroom. He'd had a private chat with Jesse, but although he had come away from it somewhat reassured—doubtless about the fact that Jesse obviously hadn't the slightest interest in me, amorously speaking—he still grew noticeably uncomfortable whenever Jesse's name came up, so I tried to mention it only when I absolutely had to. Now, I figured, was one of those times.

"Jesse told me he felt a great, um, stirring out there." I put down the paper and pointed up, for want of a better direction. "An angry one. Apparently, we have some unhappy campers somewhere. He said they're looking for someone. At first I figured he couldn't mean these guys"—I tapped the paper—

"because all they seemed to be looking for was beer. But it's possible they have another agenda." A more murderous one, I thought, but didn't say out loud.

But Father Dom, as he often did, seemed to read my thoughts.

"Good heavens, Susannah," he said, looking up from the Gameboy screen. "You can't be thinking that these young people you saw and the stirring Jesse felt have anything to do with one another, can you? Because I must say, I find that highly unlikely. From what I understand, the Angels were just that...true beacons in their community."

Jeez. Beacons. I wondered if there was anybody who'd ever refer to *me* as a beacon after I was dead. I highly doubted it. Not even my mother would go that far.

I kept my feelings to myself, however. I knew from experience that Father D wasn't going to like what I was thinking, let alone believe it. Instead, I said, "Well, just keep your eyes open, will you? Let me know if you see them around. The, er, Angels, I mean."

"Of course." Father Dom shook his head. "What a tragedy. Poor souls. So innocent. So young. Oh. Oh, my." He sheepishly held up the Gameboy. "High score."

That's when I decided I'd spent quite enough time in the principal's office for one day. Gina, who attended my old school back in Brooklyn, had a different spring break from the Mission Academy's, so while she was getting to spend her vacation in California, she had to endure a few days following me around from class to class—at least until I could figure out a way for us to ditch without getting caught.

Gina was back in world civ with Mr. Walden, and I hadn't any doubt that she was getting into all sorts of trouble while I was gone.

"All righty then," I said, getting up. "Let me know if you hear anything more about those kids."

"Yes, yes," Father Dominic said, his attention riveted to the Gameboy once again. "Bye for now."

As I left his office, I could have sworn I heard him say a bad word after the Gameboy let out a warning beep. But that would have been so unlike him, I must have heard wrong.

Yeah. Right.

CHAPTER

4

When I got back to world civ, Kelly Prescott, my friend Adam, Rob Kelleher—one of the class jocks, and a good buddy of Dopey's—and this quiet kid whose name I could never remember were just finishing up their presentation on the Nuclear Arms Race: Who Will Come in First?

It was a bogus assignment, if you asked me. I mean, with the fall of communism in Russia, who even cared?

I guess that was the point. We *should* care. Because as the charts Kelly's group was holding up revealed, there were some countries who had way more bombs and stuff than we did.

"Okay," Kelly was saying, as I came in and laid my hall pass on Mr. Walden's desk before going to my seat. "Like, as you can see, the U.S. is pretty well stocked for missiles, and stuff, but as far as tanks, the Chinese have been way better at building up their military—" Kelly pointed to a bunch of little red bombs on her chart. "And they could totally annihilate us if they wanted to."

"Except," Adam pointed out, "that there are more privately owned handguns in America than there are in the whole of the Chinese army, so—"

"So what?" Kelly demanded. I could sense that there was some division amongst the ranks of this particular group. "What good are handguns against tanks? I am so sure we are all going to stand around and shoot off our handguns at the tanks the Chinese are running us over with."

Adam rolled his eyes. He hadn't exactly been thrilled to be assigned to a group with Kelly.

"Yeah," Rob said.

The grade for the group projects was split, with thirty percent counting toward participation. I guess that "Yeah" had been Rob's contribution.

The kid whose name I didn't know didn't say anything. He was a tall, skinny kid with glasses. He had the kind of pasty white skin that made it obvious he didn't get to the beach much. The Palm Pilot in his shirt pocket revealed why.

Gina, who was sitting behind me, leaned forward and presented me with a note, written on a page of the spiral notebook in which she'd been doodling.

Where the hell have you been? she wanted to know

I picked up a pen and wrote back, *I told you. Principal wanted to see me.*

About what? Gina asked. *Have you been up to your old tricks again???*

I didn't blame her for asking. Let's just say that at our old school, back in Brooklyn, I'd been forced to skip class a lot. Well, what do you expect? I'd been the only mediator for all five boroughs of New York. That's a lot of ghosts! Here at least I had Father D to help out once in a while.

I wrote back, *Nothing like that. Father Dom is our student council advisor. I had to check with him about some of our recent expenditures.*

I thought this would be such a boring topic that Gina would drop it, but she totally didn't.

So? What were they? Gina demanded. *Your expenditures, I mean.*

Suddenly, the notebook was snatched from my hands. I looked up, and saw Cee Cee, who sat in front of me in homeroom and this class, and who had become my best friend since I'd moved to California, scribbling in it furiously. A few seconds later, she passed it back.

Did you hear? Cee Cee had written in her sprawling cursive. *About Michael Meducci, I mean?*

I wrote back, *I guess not. Who's Michael Meducci?*

Cee Cee, when she'd read what I'd written, made a face, and pointed at the kid standing in the front of the room, the pasty-looking one with the Palm Pilot.

Oh, I mouthed. Hey, I'd only started attending the Mission Academy two months earlier, in January. So sue me already if I didn't know everybody by name yet.

Cee Cee bent over the notebook, writing what seemed to be a novel. Gina and I exchanged glances. Gina looked amused. She seemed to find my entire West Coast existence highly entertaining.

Finally Cee Cee surrendered the notebook. In it she had scrawled, *Mike was the one driving the other car in that accident on the Pacific Coast Highway Saturday night. You know, the one where those four RLS students died.*

Whoa, I thought. It totally pays to be friends with the editor of the school paper. Somehow, Cee Cee always manages to ferret out everything about everyone.

I heard he was coming back from a friend's house, she wrote. *There was this fog, and I guess they didn't see each other until the last minute, when everybody swerved. His car went up an embankment, but theirs crashed through the railguard and plunged two hundred feet into the sea. Everyone in the other car died, but Michael escaped with just a couple of sprained ribs from when the air bag deployed.*

I looked up and stared at Mike Meducci. He didn't look like a kid who had, only just that weekend, been involved in an accident that had killed four people. He looked like a kid who'd maybe stayed up too late playing video games or participating in a *Star Wars* chatroom on the Internet. I was sitting too far away to tell if his fingers, holding onto the chart, were shaking, but there was something about the strained expression on his face that suggested to me that they were.

It's especially tragic, Cee Cee scribbled, *when you consider the fact that only last month, his little sister—you don't know her; she's in eighth—almost drowned at some pool party and has been in a coma ever since. Talk about a family curse....*

"So, in conclusion," Kelly said, not even attempting to make it look like she wasn't reading off an index card, and rushing her words all together so you could hardly tell what she was saying, "America-needs-to-spend-way-more-money-building-up-its-military-because-we-have-fallen-way-behind-the-Chinese-and-they-could-attack-us-any-time-they-wanted-to-thank-you."

Mr. Walden had been sitting with his feet propped up on his desk, staring over the tops of our heads at the sea, which you can see quite plainly through the windows of most of the classrooms at the Mission Academy. Now, hearing the sudden hush that fell over the classroom, he started, and dropped his feet to the floor.

"Very nice, Kelly," he said, even though it was obvious he hadn't listened to a word she'd been saying. "Anybody have questions for Kelly? Okay, great, next group—"

Then Mr. Walden blinked at me. "Um," he said, in a strange voice. "Yes?"

Since I hadn't raised my hand, or in any way indicated that I had anything to say, I was somewhat taken aback by this. Then a voice behind me said, "Um, I'm sorry, but that conclusion—that we, as a country, need to start building up our military arsenal in order to compete with the Chinese—sounds grossly ill conceived to me."

I turned around slowly in my chair to stare at Gina. She had a perfectly straight expression on her face. Still, I knew her:

She was bored. This was the kind of thing Gina did when she was bored.

Mr. Walden sat up eagerly in his chair and said, "It seems that Miss Simon's guest disagrees with the conclusion you all have come up with, Group Seven. How would you like to respond?"

"Ill conceived in what way?" Kelly demanded, not consulting with any of the other members of her group.

"Well, I just think the money you're talking about would be better spent on other things," Gina said, "besides making sure we have as many tanks as the Chinese. I mean, who cares if they have more tanks than we do? It's not like they're going to be able to drive them over to the White House and say, 'Okay, surrender now, capitalist pigs.' I mean, there's a pretty big ocean between us, right?"

Mr. Walden was practically clapping his hands with glee. "So how do you suggest the money be better spent, Miss Augustin?"

Gina shrugged. "Well, on education, of course."

"What good," Kelly wanted to know, "is an education, when you've got a tank bearing down on you?"

Adam, standing beside Kelly, rolled his eyes expressively. "Maybe," he ventured, "if we educate future generations better, they'd be able to avoid war altogether, through creative diplomacy and intelligent dialogue with their fellow man."

"Yeah," Gina said. "What he said."

"Excuse me, but are you all on crack?" Kelly wanted to know.

Mr. Walden threw a piece of chalk in Group Seven's direction. It hit their chart with a loud noise, and bounced off. This was not unusual behavior on Mr. Walden's part. He frequently threw chalk when he felt we were not paying proper attention, particularly after lunch when we were all somewhat dazed from having ingested too many corn dogs.

What was not usual, however, was Mike Meducci's reaction when the chalk hit the poster board he was holding. He let go of the chart with a yell, and ducked—actually ducked, with his hands up over his face—as if a Chinese tank was rolling toward him.

Mr. Walden did not notice this. He was still too enraged.

"Your assignment," he bellowed at Kelly, " was to make a persuasive argument. Demanding to know whether detractors of your position are on crack is not arguing persuasively."

"But seriously, Mr. Walden," Kelly said, "if they would just look at the chart, they'd see that the Chinese have way more tanks than we do, and all the education in the world isn't going to change that—"

It was at this point that Mr. Walden noticed Mike coming out of his defensive hunch.

"Meducci," he said flatly. "What's with you?"

Mr. Walden, I realized, did not know how Mike had spent his weekend. Maybe he didn't know about the comatose sister, either. How Cee Cee had managed to find out these things that even our teachers did not know was always a mystery to me.

"N-nothing," Mike stammered, looking pastier than ever. There was something weird about his expression, too. I couldn't put my finger on what, exactly, was wrong with it, but something more than just typical geek embarrassment. "S-sorry, Mr. W-Walden."

Scott Turner, one of Dopey's friends, seated a few desks away from me, muttered, "S-sorry, Mr. W-Walden," in a whispered falsetto, but still audibly enough for him to be heard by everyone in the room—especially by Michael, whose pale face actually got a little bit of color into it as the snickers reached him.

As vice president of the sophomore class, it is my duty to instill discipline in my fellow classmates during student council meetings. But I take my executive responsibilities quite seriously, and tend to correct the behavior of my more rambunctious peers whenever I feel it necessary to do so, not just during assemblies of the student council.

So I leaned over and hissed, "Hey, Scott."

Scott, still laughing at his own joke, looked over at me. And stopped laughing abruptly.

I'm not exactly sure what I was going to say—it was going to have something to do with Scott's last date with Kelly Prescott and a pair of tweezers—but Mr. Walden unfortunately beat me to it.

"Turner," he bellowed. "I want a thousand-word essay on the battle at Gettysburg on my desk in the morning. Group Eight, be prepared to give your report tomorrow. Class dismissed."

There is no bell system at the Mission Academy. We change classes on the hour, and are supposed to do so quietly. All of the classroom doors at the Mission Academy open into arched breezeways that look out into a beautiful courtyard containing all these really tall palm trees and this fountain and a statue of the Mission's founder, Junipero Serra. The Mission, being something like three hundred years old, attracts a lot of tourists, and the courtyard is the highlight of their tour, after the basilica.

The courtyard is actually one of my favorite

places to sit and meditate about stuff like...oh, I don't know: how I've had the misfortune to be born a mediator, and not a normal girl, and why I can't seem to get Jesse to like me, you know, in that special way. The sound of the bubbling fountain, the chirping of the sparrows in the rafters of the breezeway, the buzz of hummingbird wings around the plate-sized hibiscus blossoms, the hushed chatter of the tourists—who feel the grandeur of the place, and lower their voices accordingly—all made the Mission courtyard a restful place to sit and ponder one's destiny.

It was also, however, a favorite place for novices to stand and wait for innocent students to slip up by talking too loudly between classes.

No novice has ever been created that could keep Gina quiet, however.

"Dude, that was so bogus," she complained loudly as we walked toward my locker. "What kind of conclusion was *that?* I am so sure the Chinese are going to come rolling over here in tanks and attack us. How are they going to get here, anyway? By way of Canada?"

I tried not to laugh, but it was hard. Gina was outraged.

"I know that girl is your class president," she went on, "but talk about dumb blondes...."

Cee Cee, who'd been walking beside us, growled, "Watch it." Not, as I'd thought, because, being an albino, Cee Cee is the blondest of blondes, but because a novice was staring daggers at us from the courtyard.

"Oh, good, it's you," Gina said when she noticed Cee Cee, completely missing her warning glance at the novice, and not lowering her voice a bit. "Simon, Cee Cee here says she's going to the mall after school."

"My mom's birthday," Cee Cee explained apologetically. She knows how I feel about malls. Gina, who'd always had something of a selective memory, had apparently forgotten. "Gotta get her some perfume or a book or something."

"What do you say?" Gina asked me. "You want to go with her? I've never been to a real California mall. I want to check it out."

"You know," I said as I worked the combination to my locker door, "the Gap sells the same old stuff all over the country."

"Hello," Gina said. "Who cares about the Gap? I'm talking about hotties."

"Oh." I got rid of my world civ book, and fished out my bio, which I had next. "Sorry. I forgot."

"That's the problem with you, Simon," Gina said, leaning against the locker next to mine. "You don't think enough about guys."

I slammed my locker door closed. "I think a lot about guys."

"No, you don't." Gina looked at Cee Cee. "Has she even been out with one since she got here?"

"Sure, she has," Cee Cee said. "Bryce Martinson."

"No," I said.

Cee Cee looked up at me. She was a little shorter than me. "What do you mean, no?"

"Bryce and I never actually went out," I explained, a little uncomfortably. "You remember, he broke his collar bone—"

"Oh, yeah," Cee Cee said. "In that freak accident

with the crucifix. And then he transferred to another school."

Yeah, because that freak accident hadn't been an accident at all: the ghost of his dead girlfriend had dropped that crucifix on him, in a totally unfair effort to keep me from going out with him.

Which unfortunately had worked.

Then Cee Cee said, brightly, "But you definitely went out with Tad Beaumont. I saw you two together at the Coffee Clutch."

Gina, excited, asked, "Really? Simon went out with a guy? Describe."

Cee Cee frowned. "Gee," she said. "It didn't end up lasting very long, did it, Suze? There was some accident with his uncle, or something, and Tad had to go live with relatives in San Francisco."

Translation: After I'd stopped Tad's uncle, a psychotic serial killer, from murdering us both, Tad moved away with his father.

That's gratitude for you, huh?

"Gosh," Cee Cee said, thoughtfully. "Bad things seem to happen to the guys you go out with, huh, Suze?"

Suddenly feeling a little depressed, I said, "Not all of them," thinking of Jesse. Then I remembered that Jesse:

(a) was dead, so only I could see him—hardly good boyfriend material—and

(b) had never actually asked me out, so you couldn't exactly say we were dating.

It was right about then that something whizzed by us so fast, it was only a khaki blur, followed by the faintest trace of slightly familiar-smelling men's cologne. I looked around and saw that the blur had been Dopey. He was holding Michael Meducci in a headlock while Scott Turner shoved a finger in his face and snarled, "*You*'re writing that essay for me, Meducci. Got that? A thousand words on Gettysburg by tomorrow morning. And don't forget to double-space it."

I don't know what came over me. Sometimes I am simply seized by impulses over which I have not the slightest control.

But suddenly I'd shoved my books at Gina and stalked over to where my stepbrother stood. A second later I held a pinchful of the short hairs at the back of his neck.

"Let him go," I said, twisting the tiny hairs hard. This method of torture, I'd discovered recently, was much more effective than my former technique of punching Dopey in the gut. He had, over the past few weeks, greatly built up the muscles in his abdominal wall, undoubtedly as a defense against just this sort of occasion.

The only way he could keep me from grabbing him by the short hairs, however, was to shave his head, and this had apparently not occurred to him.

Dopey, opening his mouth to let out a wail, released Michael right away. Michael staggered away, scurrying to pick up the books he'd dropped.

"Suze," Dopey cried, "let go of me!"

"Yeah," Scott said. "This doesn't concern you, Simon."

"Oh, yes, it does," I said. "Everything that happens at this school concerns me. Want to know why?"

Dopey already knew the answer. I had drilled it into him on several previous occasions.

"Because you're the vice president," he said. "Now let me freakin' go, or I swear I'll tell Dad—"

I let him go, but only because Sister Ernestine showed up. The novice had apparently run for her. It's become official Mission Academy policy to send for backup whenever fights break out between Dopey and me.

"Is there a problem, Miss Simon?"

Sister Ernestine, the vice principal, is a very large woman, who wears an enormous cross between her equally sizeable breasts. She has an uncanny ability to evoke terror wherever she goes, merely by frowning. It is a talent I admire and hope to emulate someday.

"No, Sister," I said.

Sister Ernestine turned her attention toward Dopey. "Mr. Ackerman? Problem?"

Sullenly, Dopey massaged the back of his neck. "No, Sister," he said.

"Good," Sister Ernestine said. "I'm glad the two of you are finally getting along so nicely. Such sibling affection is an inspiration to us all. Now hurry along to class, please."

I turned and joined Cee Cee and Gina, who'd stood watching the whole thing.

"Jesus, Simon," Gina said with disgust as we headed into the bio lab. "No wonder the guys around here don't like you."

CHAPTER 5

"Girl," Gina said. "That is so you."

Cee Cee looked down at the outfit Gina had talked her into purchasing, then had goaded Cee Cee into putting on for our inspection.

"I don't know," she said, dubiously.

"It's you," Gina said, again. "I'm telling you. It's so you. Tell her, Suze."

"It's pretty flicking," I said truthfully. Gina had the touch. She had turned Cee Cee from fashion challenged to fashion plate.

"But you won't be able to wear it to school," I couldn't help pointing out. "It's too short." I'd learned the hard way that the Mission Academy's dress code, while fairly lenient, did not condone miniskirts under any circumstances. And I highly doubted Sister Ernestine would approve of Cee Cee's new, navel-revealing faux-fur-trimmed sweater, either.

"Where am I going to wear it, then?" Cee Cee wanted to know.

"Church," I answered with a shrug.

Cee Cee gave me a very sarcastic look. I said, "Oh, all right. Well, you can definitely wear it to the Coffee Clutch. And to parties."

Cee Cee's gaze, behind the violet lenses of her glasses, was tolerant. "I don't get invited to parties, Suze," she reminded me.

"You can always wear it to my house," Adam offered helpfully. The startled look Cee Cee threw him pretty much assured me that however much she'd spent on the outfit—and it had to have cost several months' allowance, at least—it had been worth it: Cee Cee had had a secret crush on Adam McTavish for as long as I'd known her, and probably much longer than that.

"All right, Simon," Gina said, lowering herself into one of the hard plastic chairs that littered the food court. "What were you up to while I was coordinating Ms. Webb's spring wardrobe?"

I held up my bag from Music Town. "I bought a CD," I said lamely.

Gina, appalled, echoed, "A *what?*"

"A CD." I hadn't even wanted to buy one, but sent out into the wilds of the mall with instructions to return with a new purchase, I had panicked, and headed into the first store I saw.

"You know malls give me sensory overload," I said, by way of explanation.

Gina shook her head at me, her copper curls swaying. "You can't really get mad at her," she said to Adam. "She's just so cute."

Adam shifted his attention from Cee Cee's sassy new outfit to me. "Yeah," he said. "She is." Then his gaze slipped past me, and his eyes widened. "But here come some people I'm not sure will agree."

I turned my head and saw Sleepy and Dopey sauntering toward us. The mall was like Dopey's second home, but what Sleepy was doing here, I could not imagine. All of his free time, between school and delivering pizzas—he was saving up for a Camaro—was usually spent surfing. Or sleeping.

Then he slumped down into a chair near Gina's, and said, in a voice I'd never heard him use before, "Hey, I heard you were here."

Suddenly all became clear.

"Hey," I said to Cee Cee, who was still gazing rapturously in Adam's direction. She was trying to figure out, I could tell, just what precisely he'd meant when he'd said she could wear her new outfit to his house. Had he been sexually harassing her—as she clearly hoped—or merely making conversation?

"Yeah?" Cee Cee asked. She didn't even bother to turn her head in my direction.

I grimaced. I could see I was all alone on this one.

"You got your mom's present yet?" I demanded.

Cee Cee said, faintly, "No."

"Good." I dropped my CD into her lap. "Hang onto this. I'll go get her Oprah's latest pick of the month. How about that?"

"That sounds great," Cee Cee said, still without so much as a glance at me, although she did wave a twenty in the air.

Rolling my eyes, I snatched the bill, then stomped off before I burst a blood vessel from screaming as hard as I could. You'd have screamed, too, if you'd seen what I had as I left the food court, which was

Dopey trying desperately to squeeze a chair in between Sleepy and Gina.

I don't get it. I really don't. I mean, I know I probably come off as insensitive and maybe even a little weird, what with the mediator thing, but deep down, I am really a caring person. I am very fair minded and intelligent, and sometimes I'm even funny. And I know I'm not a dog. I mean, I fully blow-dry my hair every morning, and I have been told on more than one occasion (okay, by my mom, but it still counts) that my eyes are like emeralds. So what gives? How come Gina has *two* guys vying for her attention, while I can't even get one? I mean, even dead guys don't seem to like me so much, and I don't think they have a whole lot of options.

I was still mulling over this in the bookstore as I stood in line for the cashier, the book for Cee Cee's mother in my hands. That was when something brushed my shoulder. I turned around and found myself staring at Michael Meducci.

"Um," he said. He was holding a book on computer programming. He looked, in the fluorescent lights of the bookstore, pastier than ever. "Hi." He touched his glasses nervously, as if to assure himself they were still there. "I thought that was you."

I said, "Hi, Michael," and moved up a space in the line.

Michael moved up with me. "Oh," he said. "You know my name." He sounded pleased.

I didn't point out that up until that day, I hadn't. I just said, "Yeah," and smiled.

Maybe the smile was a mistake. Because Michael stepped a little closer, and gushed, "I just wanted to say thanks. You know. For what you did to your, um, stepbrother today. You know. To make him let me go."

"Yeah," I said again. "Well, don't worry about it."

"No, I mean it. Nobody has ever done anything like that for me—I mean, before you came to school at the Mission, no one ever stood up to Brad Ackerman. He got away with everything. With murder, practically."

"Well," I said. "Not anymore."

"No," Michael said with a nervous laugh. "No, not anymore."

The person ahead of me stepped up to the cashier, and I moved into her place. Michael moved, too, only he went a little too far, and ended up colliding with me. He said, "Oh, I'm sorry," and backed up.

"That's okay," I said. I began to wish, even if it had meant risking a brain hemorrhage, that I'd stayed with Gina.

"Your hair," Michael said in a soft voice, "smells really good."

Oh, my God. I thought I was going to have an aneurism right there in line. *Your hair smells really good? Your hair smells really good?* Who did he think he was? James Bond? You don't tell someone their hair smells good. Not in a *mall.*

Fortunately, the cashier yelled, "Next," and I hurried up to pay for my purchase, thinking that by the time I turned around again, Michael would be gone.

Wrong. So wrong.

Not only was he still there, but it turned out he already owned the book on computer programming—

he was just *carrying it around*—so he didn't even have to make a stop at the cashier's counter...which was where I'd planned on ditching him.

No. Oh, no. Instead, he followed me right out of the store.

Okay, I told myself. The guy's sister is in a coma. She went to a pool party, and ended up on life support. That's gotta screw a person up. And what about the car accident? The guy was just in a horrifying car accident. It's entirely possible that he may have killed four people. Four people! Not on purpose, of course. But four people, dead, while you yourself escaped perfectly unscathed. That and the comatose sister... well, that's gotta give a guy issues, right?

So cut him a little slack. Be a little nice to him.

The trouble was that I had already been a little nice to him, and look what had happened: he was practically stalking me.

Michael followed me right into Victoria's Secret, where I'd instinctively headed, thinking no boy would follow a girl into a place where bras were on such prominent display. Boy, was I ever wrong.

"So, what'd you think," Michael wanted to know as I stood there fingering a cheetah print number in rayon, "about our group report? Do you agree with your, uh, friend that Kelly's argument was fatuous?"

Fatuous? What sort of word was *that?*

A saleslady came up to us before I had a chance to reply. "Hello," she said, brightly. "Have you noticed our sales table? Buy three pairs of panties, get a fourth pair free."

I couldn't believe she'd said the word *panties* in front of Michael. And I couldn't believe that Michael just kept standing there *smiling!* I couldn't even say the word *panties* in front of my *mother!* I whirled around and headed out of the store.

"I don't normally come to the mall," Michael was saying. He was sticking to me like a leech. "But when I heard you were going to be here, well, I thought I'd come over and see what it's all about. Do you come here a lot?"

I was trying to head in the general direction of the food court, in the vague hope that I might be able to ditch Michael in the throng in front of Chick Fill-A. It was tough going, though. For one thing, it looked as if just about every kid in the peninsula had decided to go to the mall after school. And for another, the mall had had one of those events, you know, that malls are always having. This one had been some kind of screwed-up mardi gras, with floats and gold masks and necklaces and all. I guess it had been a success, since they'd left a lot of the stuff up, like these big shiny purple and gold puppets. Bigger than life size, the puppets were suspended from the mall's glass atrium ceiling. Some of them were fifteen or twenty feet long. Their appendages dangled down in what I suppose was intended to be a whimsical manner, but in some cases made it hard to maneuver through the crowds.

"No," I said in reply to Michael's question. "I try never to come here. I hate it."

Michael brightened. "Really?" he gushed, as a wave of middle schoolers poured around him. "Me, too! Wow, that's really a coincidence. You know, there aren't a whole lot of people our age who dislike places like this. Man is a social animal, you know, and as such is usually drawn toward areas of congregation. It's really an indication of some biological dysfunction that you and I aren't enjoying ourselves."

It occurred to me that my youngest stepbrother, Doc, and Michael Meducci had a lot in common.

It also occurred to me that pointing out to a girl that she might be suffering from a biological dysfunction was not exactly the way to win her heart.

"Maybe," Michael said, as we dodged a large puppet hand dangling down from an insanely grinning puppet head some fifteen feet above us, "you and I could go somewhere a bit quieter. I have my mom's car. We could go get coffee or something, in town, if you want—"

That's when I heard it. A familiar giggle.

Don't ask me how I could have heard it over the chatter of the people all around us, and the piped-in mall Muzak, and the screaming of some kid whose mother wouldn't let him have any ice cream. I just heard it, is all.

Laughter. The same laughter I'd heard the day before at Jimmy's, right before I'd spotted the ghosts of those four dead kids.

And then the next thing I knew, there was a loud snap—the kind of sound a rubber band that's been stretched too tightly makes when it breaks. I yelled, "Look out!" and tackled Michael Meducci, knocking him to the ground.

Good thing I did, too. Because a second later, exactly where we'd been standing, crashed a giant grinning puppet head.

When the dust settled, I lifted my face from Michael Meducci's shirtfront and stared at the thing.

It wasn't made of papier-mâché, like I'd thought. It was made of plaster. Bits of plaster were everywhere; clouds of it were still floating around, making me cough. Chunks of it had been wrenched from the puppet's face, so that, while it was still leering at me, it was doing so with only one eye and a toothless smile.

For half a beat, there was no sound whatsoever, except for my coughing and Michael's unsteady breathing.

Then a woman screamed.

All hell broke loose after that. People fell over themselves in an effort to get out from under the puppets overhead, as if all of them were going to come crashing down at once.

I guess I couldn't exactly blame them. The thing had to have weighed a couple hundred pounds, at least. If it had landed on Michael, it would have killed, or at least badly hurt, him. There was no doubt in my mind about that.

Just as there was no doubt, even before I spotted him, who owned the jeering voice that drawled a second later, "Well, look what we have here. Isn't this *cozy?*"

I looked up and saw that Dopey—along with a breathless Gina, Cee Cee, Adam, and Sleepy—had all hurried over.

I didn't even realize I was still lying on top of Michael until Sleepy reached down and pulled me off.

"Why is it," my stepbrother asked in a bored voice, "that you can't be left alone for five minutes without something collapsing on top of you?"

I glared at him as I stumbled to my feet. I have to say, I really can't wait until Sleepy goes away to college.

"Hey," Sleepy said, reaching down to give Michael's cheeks a couple of slaps, I suppose in some misguided attempt to bring him around, though I doubt this is a method espoused by EMS. Michael's eyes were closed, and even though I could see he was breathing, he didn't look good.

The slaps worked, though. Michael's eyelids fluttered open.

"You okay?" I asked him worriedly.

He didn't see the hand I stretched out toward him. He'd lost his glasses. He fumbled around for them in the plaster dust.

"M-my glasses," he said.

Cee Cee found them and picked them up, brushing them off as best she could before handing them back to him.

"Thanks." Michael put the glasses on, and his eyes, behind the lenses, got very large as he took in the carnage around us. The puppet had missed him, but it had managed to take out a bench and a steel trashcan without any problem whatsoever.

"Oh, my God," Michael said.

"I'll say," Adam said. "If it hadn't been for Suze, you'd have been crushed to death by a giant plaster puppet head. Kind of a sucky way to die, huh?"

Michael continued to stare at the debris. "Oh, my God," he said again.

"Are you all right, Suze?" Gina asked, laying a hand on my arm.

I nodded. "Yeah, I think so. No broken bones,

anyway. Michael? How about you? You still in one piece?"

"How would he be able to tell?" Dopey asked with a sneer, but I glared at him, and I guess he remembered how hard I can pull hair, since for once he shut up.

"I'm fine," Michael said. He shoved away the hands Sleepy had stretched out to help him to his feet. "Leave me alone. I said I was fine."

Sleepy backed up. "Whoa," he said. "Excuse me. Just trying to help. Come on, G. Our shakes are melting."

Wait a minute. I threw a startled glance in the direction of my best friend and eldest stepbrother. *G?* Who's *G?*

Cee Cee fished a bag out from underneath the waves of shiny purple and gold material. "Hey," she said delightedly. "Is this the book you got for my mom?"

Sleepy, I saw, was walking back toward the food court, his arm around Gina. *Gina. My best friend!* My best friend appeared to be allowing my stepbrother to buy her shakes and put his arm around her! And call her G!

Michael had climbed to his feet. Some mall cops arrived just about then and went, "Hey, there, guy, take it easy. An ambulance is on its way."

But Michael, with a violent motion, shrugged free of them, and, with a last, inscrutable look at the puppet head, stumbled away, the mall cops trailing after him, obviously concerned about the likelihood of a concussion...or a lawsuit.

"Wow," Cee Cee said, shaking her head. "That's

gratitude for you. You save the guy's life, and he takes off without even a thank you."

Adam said, "Yeah. How is it, Suze, that whenever something is about to come crashing down on some guy's head, you always know it and tackle him? And how can I get something to crash down on my head so that you have to tackle me?"

Cee Cee whacked him in the gut. Adam pretended it had hurt, and staggered around comically for a while before nearly tripping over the puppet, and then stopping to stare down at it.

"I wonder what caused it," Adam said. Some mall employees were there now, wondering the same thing, with many nervous glances in my direction. If they'd known my mom was a television news journalist, they probably would have been falling all over themselves in an attempt to give me free gift certificates to Casual Corner and stuff.

"I mean, it's kind of weird if you think about it," Adam went on. "The thing was up there for weeks, and then all of a sudden Michael Meducci stands underneath it, and—"

"Bam," Cee Cee said. "Kind of like...I don't know. Someone up there has got it out for him, or something."

Which reminded me. I looked around, thinking I might catch a glimpse of the owner of that giggle I'd heard, just before the puppet had come down on us.

I didn't see anyone, but that didn't matter. I knew who'd been behind it.

And it sure hadn't been any angel.

CHAPTER 6

"Well," Jesse said when I told him about it later that night. "You know what you have to do, don't you?"

"Yeah," I said sullenly, my chin on my knees. "I have to tell her about that time I found that nudie magazine under the front seat of the Rambler. That oughtta make her change her mind about him real quick."

The scarred eyebrow went up. "Susannah," he said. "What are you talking about?"

"Gina," I said, surprised he didn't know. "And Sleepy."

"No," Jesse said. "I meant about the boy, Susannah."

"What boy?" Then I remembered. "Oh. You mean Michael?"

"Yes," Jesse said. "If what you're telling me is true, he is in a lot of danger, Susannah."

"I know." I leaned back on my elbows. The two of us were sitting out on the roof of the front porch, which happened to stick out beneath my bedroom windows. It was kind of nice out there, actually, under the stars. We were high enough up so that no one could see us—not that anyone but me and Father Dom could see Jesse, anyway—and it smelled good because of the giant pine tree to one side of the porch. It was the only place, these days, that we could sit and talk without fear of being interrupted by people. Well, just one person, actually: my houseguest, Gina.

"So, what are you going to do about it?" In the moonlight, Jesse's white shirt looked blue. So did the highlights in his black hair.

"I have no idea," I said.

"Don't you?"

Jesse looked at me. I hate it when he does that. It makes me feel...I don't know. Like he's mentally comparing me with someone else. And the only someone else I could think of was Maria de Silva, the girl Jesse was on his way to marry when he died. I had seen a portrait of her once. She was one hot babe, for the 1850s. It's no fun, let me tell you, being compared to a chick who died before you were even born.

And always had a hoop skirt to hide the size of her butt under.

"You're going to have to find them," Jesse said. "The Angels. Because if I'm right, that boy will not be safe until they are persuaded to move on."

I sighed. Jesse was right. Jesse was always right. It was just that tracking down a bunch of partying ghosts was so not what I wanted to be doing while Gina was in town.

On the other hand, hanging around with me was not exactly proving to be what Gina wanted to do.

I stood up and walked carefully across the roof tiles, then stooped to peer through the bay windows into my bedroom. The daybed was empty. I picked my way back down to where Jesse was sitting, and slumped down beside him again.

"Jeez," I said. "She's still in there."

Jesse looked down at me, the moonlight playing around the little smile on his face. "You cannot blame her," he said, "for being interested in your brother."

"Stepbrother," I reminded him. "And yes, I can. He's vermin. And he's got her in his lair."

Jesse's smile grew broader. Even his teeth, in the moonlight, looked blue. "They are only playing computer games, Susannah."

"How do you know?" Then I remembered. He was a ghost. He could go anywhere. "Well, sure. The last time you looked, maybe. Who knows what they're doing now?"

Jesse sighed. "Do you want me to look again?"

"*No.*" I was horrified. "I don't care what she does. If she wants to hang around with a big loser like Sleepy, I can't stop her."

"Brad was there, too," Jesse pointed out. "Last time I looked."

"Oh, great. So she's hanging out with two losers."

"I don't understand why you are so unhappy about it," Jesse said. He had stretched out across the tiles, contented as I'd ever seen him. "I like it much better this way."

"What way?" I groused. I couldn't get quite as comfortable. I kept finding prickly pine needles beneath my butt.

"Just the two of us," he said with a shrug. "Like it's always been."

Before I had a chance to reply to what—to me, anyway—seemed an extraordinarily heartfelt and perhaps even romantic admission, headlights flashed in the driveway, and Jesse looked past me.

"Who's that?"

I didn't look. I didn't care. I said, "One of Sleepy's friends, I'm sure. What was that you were saying? About how you like it being just the two of us?"

But Jesse was squinting through the darkness. "This is not a friend of Jake's," he said. "Not bringing with him so much...fear. Could this be the boy, Michael, perhaps?"

"What?"

I swung around and, clinging to the edge of the roof, watched as a minivan pulled up the driveway and parked behind my mother's car.

A second later, Michael Meducci got out from behind the wheel, and with a nervous glance at my front door, began heading toward it, his expression determined.

"Oh, my God," I cried, reeling back from the roof's edge. "You're right! It's him! What do I do?"

Jesse only shook his head at me. "What do you mean, what do you do? You know what to do. You've done this hundreds of times before." When I only continued to stare at him, he leaned forward, until his face was just a couple of inches from mine.

But instead of kissing me like I'd hoped, for one wild heart-pounding moment, he would, he said, enunciating distinctly, "You're a mediator, Susannah. Go mediate."

I opened my mouth to inform him that I highly doubted Michael was at my house because he wanted help with his poltergeist problem, considering he couldn't know I was in the ghostbusting business. It was much more likely that he was here to ask me out. On a date. Something that I was sure had never occurred to Jesse, since they probably didn't have dates back when he'd been alive, but which happened to girls in the twenty-first century with alarming regularity. Well, not to me, necessarily, but to most girls, anyway.

I was about to point out that this was going to ruin our wonderful opportunity to be alone together when the doorbell rang, and deep inside the house, I heard Doc yell, "I'll get it!"

"Oh, God," I said, and dropped my head down into my hands.

"Susannah," Jesse said. There was concern in his voice. "Are you all right?"

I shook myself. What was I thinking? Michael Meducci was not at my house to ask me out. If he'd wanted to ask me out, he would have called like a normal person. No, he was here for some other reason. I had nothing to worry about. Nothing at all.

"I'm fine," I said, and got slowly to my feet.

"You don't sound fine," Jesse said.

"I'm fine," I said. I started crawling back into my room, through the open window Spike used.

I had wiggled most of the way in when the inevitable thump on my door occurred. "Enter," I said from where I lay, collapsed against the window seat, and Doc opened the door and stuck his head into my room.

"Hey, Suze," he whispered. "There's a *guy* here to see you. I think it's that guy you all were talking about at dinner. You know, the guy from the mall."

"I know," I said to the ceiling.

"Well," Doc said, fidgeting a little. "What should I do? I mean, your mom sent me up here to tell you. Should I say you're in the shower, or something?" Doc's voice became a little dry. "That's what girls always have their brothers say when my friends and I try calling them."

I turned my head and looked at Doc. If I'd had to choose one Ackerman brother to be stuck with on a desert island, Doc would definitely have been my pick. Red haired and freckle faced, he hadn't quite grown into his enormous ears yet, but at only twelve he was by far the smartest of my stepbrothers.

The thought of any girl making up an excuse to avoid talking to him made my blood boil.

His statement tweaked my conscience. Of course I wasn't going to make up an excuse. Michael Meducci may be a geek. And he may not have acted with any real class earlier that day at the mall. But he was still a human being.

I guess.

I said, "Tell him I'll be right down."

Doc look visibly relieved. He grinned, revealing a mouthful of sparkling braces. "Okay," he said, and disappeared.

I climbed slowly to my feet, and sauntered over to the mirror above my dressing table. California had greatly improved both my complexion and my hair. My skin—only slightly tanned thanks to SPF 15 sunblock—looked fine without any makeup, and I'd given up trying to straighten my long brown hair, and simply let it curl. A single hit of lip gloss, and I was on my way. I didn't bother changing out of my cargo pants and T-shirt. I didn't want to overwhelm the guy, after all.

Michael was waiting for me in the living room, his hands shoved in his pants pockets, looking at the many school portraits of me and my stepbrothers that hung upon the wall. My stepfather was sitting in a chair he never sat in, talking to Michael. When I walked in he dried up, then climbed to his feet.

"Well," Andy said after a few seconds of silence. "I'll just leave the two of you alone, then." Then he left the room, even though I could tell he didn't want to. Which was kind of strange, since Andy usually takes only the most perfunctory interest in my affairs, except when they happen to involve the police.

"Suze," Michael said when Andy was gone. I smiled at him encouragingly since he looked like he was about to expire from nervousness.

"Hey, Mike," I said easily. "You okay? No permanent injury?"

He said with a smile that I suppose he meant to match mine, but which was actually pretty wan, "No permanent injury. Except to my pride."

In an effort to diffuse some of the nervous energy in the room, I flopped down onto one of my mom's armchairs—the one with the Pottery Barn slipcover she was always yelling at the dog for sleeping on—and said, "Hey, it wasn't your fault the mall authority did a shoddy job of hanging up their mardi gras decorations."

I watched him carefully to see how he replied. Did he know? I wondered.

Michael sank into the armchair across from mine. "That's not what I meant," he said. "I meant that I'm ashamed of the way I acted today. Instead of thanking you, I—well, I behaved ungraciously, and I just came by to apologize. I hope you'll forgive me."

He didn't know. He didn't know why that puppet had come down on him, or he was the best damned actor I'd ever seen.

"Um," I said. "Sure. I forgive you. No problem."

Oh, but it was a problem. To Michael, it was apparently a great big problem.

"It's just that—" Michael got up out of the chair and started pacing around the living room. Our house is the oldest one in the neighborhood—there's even a bullet hole in one of the walls, left over from when Jesse had been alive, when our house was a haven for gamblers and gold rushers and fiancés on their way to meet their brides. Andy had rebuilt it almost from scratch—except for the bullet hole, which he'd framed—but the floorboards still creaked a little under Michael's feet as he paced.

"It's just that something happened to me this weekend," Michael said to the fireplace, "and ever since then...well, strange things have been happening."

So he did know. He knew *something*, anyway. This was a relief. It meant I didn't have to tell him.

"Things like that puppet falling down on you?" I asked, even though I already knew the answer.

"Yeah," Michael said. "And other things, too." He shook his head. "But I don't want to burden you with my problems. I feel badly enough about what happened."

"Hey," I said with a shrug. "You were shaken up. It's understandable. No hard feelings. Listen, about what happened to you this weekend, do you want to—"

"No." Michael, usually the quietest of people, spoke with a forcefulness I'd never heard him use before. "It's not understandable," he said vehemently. "It's not understandable, and it's not excusable, either. Suze, you already—I mean, that thing with Brad earlier today—"

I stared at him blankly. I had no idea what he was getting at. Although, looking back on it, I should have. I really should have.

"And then when you saved my life at the mall....It's just that I was trying so hard, you know, to show you that that's not who I am—the kind of guy who needs a girl to fight his battles for him. And then you did it *again....*"

My mouth dropped open. This was not going at all the way it was supposed to go.

"Michael," I began, but he held up a hand.

"No," he said. "Let me finish. It's not that I'm not grateful, Suze. It's not that I don't appreciate what you're trying to do for me. It's just that...I really like you, and if you would agree to go out with me this Friday night, I'll show you that I am not the sniveling coward I've acted like so far in our relationship."

I stared at him. It was as if the gears in my mind had slowed suddenly to a halt. I couldn't think. I couldn't think what to do. All I could think was, *Relationship?* What *relationship?*

"I've already asked your father," Michael said from where he stood in the center of our living room. "And he said it was all right as long as you were home by eleven."

My father? He'd asked my *father?* I had a sudden picture of Michael talking to my dad, who'd died over a decade earlier, but who frequently shows up in ghost form to torture me about my bad driving skills, and other things like that. He'd have gotten an enormous kick, I knew, out of Michael—one I'd never likely hear the end of.

"Your stepfather, I mean," Michael corrected himself, as if he'd read my thoughts.

But how could he have read my thoughts when they were in such confusion? Because this was wrong. It was all wrong. It wasn't supposed to go like this. Michael was supposed to tell me about the car accident, and then I would say, in a kind voice, that I already knew. Then I'd warn him about the ghosts, and he either wouldn't believe me, or he'd be eternally grateful, and that would be the end of it—except, of course, I'd still have to find the RLS Angels and quell their murderous wrath before they managed to get their mitts on him again.

That's how it was *supposed* to go. He wasn't supposed to *ask me out.* Asking me out was not part of the program. At least, it had never gone like that before.

I opened my mouth—not in astonishment this time, but to say, *Gee, no, Michael, I'm sorry, but I'm busy this Friday...and every Friday for the rest of my life, incidentally*—when a familiar voice beside me said, quickly, "Think before you say no, Susannah."

I turned my head, and saw Jesse sitting in the armchair Michael had vacated.

"He needs your help, Susannah," Jesse went on, swiftly, in his deep, low voice. "He is in very grave danger from the spirits of those he killed—however accidentally. And you are not going to be able to protect him from a distance. If you alienate him now, he'll never let you close enough to help him later when he's really going to need you."

I narrowed my eyes at Jesse. I couldn't say anything to him, of course, because Michael would hear me and think I was talking to myself, or worse. But what I really wanted to say was, Look, this is taking everything a little too far, don't you think?

But I couldn't say that. Because, I realized, Jesse was right. The only way I was going to be able to keep an eye on the Angels was by keeping an eye on Michael.

I heaved a sigh, and said, "Yeah, okay. Friday's fine."

I won't describe what Michael said after that. The whole thing was just too excruciatingly embarrassing for words. I tried to remind myself that this was probably what Bill Gates was like in high school, and look at him now. I bet all the girls who knew him back then are really kicking themselves now for having turned down his invitations to prom, or whatever.

But to tell you the truth, it didn't do much good. Even if he had a trillion dollars like Bill Gates, I still wouldn't let Michael Meducci put his tongue in my mouth.

Michael left eventually, and I made my way

grumpily back up the stairs—well, after enduring an interrogation from my mother, who came out as soon as she heard the front door close and demanded to know who Michael's parents were, where he lived, where we'd be going on our date, and why wasn't I more excited? A boy had asked me out!

Returning at last to my room, I noticed that Gina was back. She was lying on the daybed, pretending to read a magazine, and acting like she had no idea where I'd been. I walked over, snatched it away from her, and hit her over the head with it a few times.

"Okay, okay," she said, throwing her arms up over her head and giggling. "So I know already. Did you say yes?"

"What was I supposed to say?" I demanded, flopping down onto my own bed. "He was practically crying."

Even as I said it, I felt disloyal. Michael's eyes, behind the lenses of his glasses, had been very bright, it was true. But he had not actually been crying. I was pretty sure.

"Oh, my God," Gina said to the ceiling. "I can't believe you're going out with a geek."

"Yeah," I said, "well, you haven't exactly been exercising much discrimination lately yourself, *G.*"

Gina rolled over onto her stomach and looked at me seriously. "Jake's not as bad as you think, Suze," she said. "He's actually very sweet."

I summed up the situation in one word: *"Ew."*

Gina, with a laugh, rolled onto her back again. "Well, so what?" she asked. "I'm on vacation. It's not like it could possibly go anywhere anyway."

"Just promise me," I said, "that you aren't going

to...I don't know. Get full frontal with one of them, or anything."

Gina just grinned some more. "What about you and the geek? You two going to be doing any lip-locking?"

I picked up one of the pillows from my bed and threw it at her. She sat up and caught it with a laugh. "What's the matter?" she wanted to know. "Isn't he The One?"

I leaned back against the rest of my pillows. Outside, I heard the familiar thump of Spike's four paws hitting the porch roof. "What one?" I asked.

"You know," Gina said. "The One. The one the psychic talked about."

I blinked at her. "What psychic? What are you talking about?"

Gina said, "Oh, come on. Madame Zara. Remember? We went to her at that school fair in like the sixth grade. And she told you about being a mediator."

"Oh." I lay perfectly still. I was worried if I moved or said anything much, I would reveal more than I wanted to. Gina knew...but only a little. Not enough to really understand.

At least, that's what I thought then.

"You don't remember what else she said?" Gina demanded. "About you, I mean? About how you were only going to have one love in your life, but that it was going to last until the end of time?"

I stared at the lace trim of the canopy that hung over my bed. I said, my throat gone mysteriously dry, "I don't remember that."

"Well, I don't think you heard much of what she

said after that bit about you being a mediator. You were in shock. Oh, look. Here comes that...cat."

Gina avoided, I noticed, supplying any descriptives for Spike, who climbed in through the open window, then stalked over to his food bowl and cried to be fed. Apparently, the memory of what had happened the last time she'd called the cat a name—the thing with the fingernail polish—was still fresh in Gina's mind. As fresh, apparently, as what that psychic had said all those years ago.

One love that would last until the end of time.

I realized, as I picked up Spike's bag of food, that my palms had broken out into a cold sweat.

"Wouldn't you die," Gina asked, "if it turned out your one true love was Michael Meducci?"

"Totally," I replied, automatically.

But it wasn't. If it was true—and I had no reason to doubt it, since Madame Zara had been right about the mediator thing, the only person in the world, with the exception of Father Dominic, who had ever guessed—then I knew perfectly well who it was.

And it wasn't Michael Meducci.

CHAPTER 7

Not that Michael didn't try.

The next morning he was waiting for me in the parking lot as Gina, Sleepy, Dopey, Doc, and I stumbled out of the Rambler and started making our way toward our various lines for assembly. Michael asked if he could carry my books. Telling myself that the RLS Angels could show up at any time and attempt to murder him again, I let him. Better to keep an eye on him, I thought, than to let him wander into God only knew what.

Still, it wasn't all that fun. Behind us, Dopey kept doing a very convincing imitation of someone throwing up.

And later, at lunch, which I traditionally spend with Adam and Cee Cee—though this particular day, since Gina was in our midst, we had been joined by her groupies, Sleepy, Dopey, and about a half dozen boys I didn't know, each of whom was vying desperately for Gina's attention—Michael asked if he could join us. Again, I had no choice but to say yes.

And then when, strolling toward the Rambler after school, it was suggested that we use the next four or five hours of daylight to its best advantage by doing our homework at the beach, Michael must have been nearby. How else could he have known to show up at the Carmel Beach, beach chair in tow, an hour later?

"Oh, God," Gina said from her beach towel. "Don't look now, but your one true love approacheth."

I looked. And stifled a groan. And rolled over to make room for him.

"Are you mental?" Cee Cee demanded, which was an interesting question coming from her, considering the fact that she was seated in the shade of a beach umbrella—no big deal, and perfectly understandable, considering the number of times she'd been taken to the hospital with sun poisoning.

But she was also wearing a rain hat—the brim of which she'd pulled well down—long pants, and a long-sleeved T. Gina, stretched out in the sun beside her like a Nubian princess, had lifted a casual brow and inquired, "Who are you supposed to be? Gilligan?"

"I mean it, Suze," Cee Cee said as Michael came nearer. "You better nip this one in the bud, and fast."

"I can't," I grumbled, shifting my textbooks over in the sand to make room for Michael and his beach chair.

"What do you mean, you *can't?*" Cee Cee inquired. "You had no trouble telling Adam to get lost these past two months. Not," she added, her gaze straying toward the waves where all the guys, including Adam, were surfing, "that I don't appreciate it."

"It's a long story," I said.

"I hope you aren't doing it because you feel sorry for him about that whole thing with his sister," Cee Cee said grumpily. "Not to mention those dead kids."

"Shut up, will you," I said. "He's coming."

And then he was there, dropping his stuff all over the place, spilling cold soda on Gina's back, and taking an inordinately long time to figure out how his beach chair worked. I bore it as well as I could, telling myself, You are all that is keeping him from becoming a geek pancake.

But I gotta tell you, it was sort of hard to believe, out there in the sun, that anything bad—like vengeance-minded ghosts—even existed. Everything was just so...right.

At least until Adam, claiming he needed a break—but really, I noticed, taking the opportunity to plunge down into the sand next to us and show off his four or five chest hairs—threw down his board. Then Michael looked up from his calculus book—he was taking senior math and science classes—and said, "Mind if I borrow that?"

Adam, the easiest going of men, shrugged and said, "Be my guest. Wave face is kinda flat, but you might be able to pick off some clean ones. Water's cold, though. Better take my suit."

Then, as Gina, Cee Cee, and I watched with mild interest, Adam unzipped his wetsuit, stepped out of it, and, dressed only in swim trunks, handed the black rubber thing to Michael, who promptly removed his glasses and stripped off his shirt.

One of Gina's hands whipped out and seized my wrist. Her fingernails bit into my skin.

"Oh, my God," she breathed.

Even Cee Cee, I noticed with a quick glance, was staring, completely transfixed, at Michael Meducci as he stepped into Adam's wetsuit and zipped it up.

"Would you," he asked, dropping to one knee in the sand beside me, "hang onto these?"

He slipped his glasses into my hands. I had a chance to look into his eyes, and noticed for the first time that they were a very deep, very bright blue.

"Sure thing," I heard myself murmur.

He smiled. Then he got back to his feet, picked up Adam's board, and, with a polite nod to us girls, trudged out into the waves.

"Oh, my God," Gina said again.

Adam, who'd collapsed into the sand beside Cee Cee, leaned up on an elbow and demanded, "What?"

When Michael had joined Sleepy, Dopey, and their other friends in the surf, Gina turned her face slowly toward mine. "Did you see that?" she asked.

I nodded dumbly.

"But that—that—" Cee Cee stammered. "That defies all logic."

Adam sat up. "What are you guys talking about?" he wanted to know.

But we could only shake our heads. Speech was impossible.

Because it turned out that Michael Meducci, underneath his pen protector, was totally and completely buff.

"He must," Cee Cee ventured, "work out like three hours a day."

"More like five," Gina murmured.

"He could bench press *me*," I said, and both Cee Cee and Gina nodded in agreement.

"Are you guys," Adam demanded, "talking about *Michael Meducci?*"

We ignored him. How could we not? For we had just seen a god—pasty skinned, it was true, but perfect in every other way.

"All he needs," Gina breathed, "is to come out from behind that computer once in a while and get a little color."

"No," I said. I couldn't bear the thought of that perfectly sculpted body marred by skin cancer. "He's fine the way he is."

"Just a little color," Gina said again. "I mean, SPF 15 and he'll still get a little brown. That's all he needs."

"No," I said again.

"Suze is right," Cee Cee said. "He's perfect the way he is."

"Oh, my God," Adam said, flopping back disgustedly into the sand. "*Michael Meducci.* I can't believe you guys are talking that way about *Michael Meducci.*"

But how could we help it? He was perfection. Okay, so he wasn't the best surfer. That, we realized, while we watched him get tossed off Adam's board by a fairly small wave that Sleepy and Dopey rode with ease, would have been asking for too much.

But in every other way, he was one hundred percent genuine hottie.

At least until he was knocked over by a middling to large-size wave and did not resurface.

At first we were not alarmed. Surfing was not something I particularly wanted to try—while I love the beach, I have no affection at all for the ocean. In fact, quite the opposite: the water scares me because there's no telling what else is swimming around in all that murky darkness. But I had watched Sleepy and Dopey ride enough waves to know that surfers often disappear for long moments, only to come popping up yards away, usually flashing a big grin and an OK sign with their thumb and index finger.

But the wait for Michael to come popping up seemed longer than usual. We saw Adam's board shoot out of a particularly large wave, and head, riderless, toward the shore. Still no sign of Michael.

This was when the lifeguard—the same big blond one who'd attempted to rescue Dopey; we had stationed ourselves close to his chair, as had become our custom—sat up straight, and suddenly lifted his binoculars to his face.

I, however, did not need binoculars to see what I saw next. And that was Michael finally breaking the surface after having been down nearly a minute. Only no sooner had he come up than he was pulled down again, and not by any undertow or riptide.

No, this I saw quite clearly: Michael was pulled down by a rope of seaweed that had somehow twined itself around his neck....

And then I saw there was no "somehow" about it. The seaweed was being held there by a pair of hands.

A pair of hands belonging to someone in the water beneath him.

Someone who had no need to surface for air. Because that someone was already dead.

Now, I'm not going to tell you that I did what I did next with any sort of conscious thought. If I'd been thinking at all, I'd have stayed exactly where I was and hoped for the best. All I can say in defense of my actions is that, after years and years of dealing with the undead, I acted purely on instinct, without thinking anything through.

Which was why, as the lifeguard was charging through the surf toward Michael, his little orange flotation device in hand, I leaped up and followed.

Now, maybe I've seen the movie *Jaws* one too many times, but I have always made it a point never to wade farther than waist-deep into the ocean—any ocean. So when I found myself surging toward the spot where I'd last seen Michael, and felt the sand shelf I'd been running on give out beneath me, I tried to tell myself that the lurch my heart gave was one of adrenaline, not fear.

I tried to tell myself that, of course. But I didn't believe me. When I realized I was going to have to start swimming, I completely freaked. I swam, all right—I know how to do that, at least. But the whole time I was thinking, Oh, my God, please don't let anything gross, like an eel, touch me on any part of my body. Please don't let a jellyfish sting me. Please don't let a shark swim up from underneath me and bite me in half.

But as it turned out, I had way worse things to worry about than eels, jellyfish, or sharks.

Behind me, I could hear voices shouting dimly. Gina and Cee Cee and Adam, I figured, in the part of my brain that wasn't paralyzed with fear. Yelling at me to get out of the water. What did I think I was doing, anyway? The lifeguard had the situation well in hand.

But the lifeguard couldn't see—or fight—the hands that were pulling Michael down.

I saw the lifeguard—who had no idea, I'm sure, that some crazy girl had dove in after him—let the enormous wave approaching us gently lift his body and propel him that much closer to where Michael had disappeared. I tried his technique, only to end up sputtering, with a mouthful of saltwater. My eyes were stinging, and my teeth starting to chatter. It was really, really cold in the water without a wetsuit.

And then, a few yards away from me, Michael suddenly resurfaced, gasping for breath and clawing at the rope of seaweed around his neck. The lifeguard, in two easy strokes, was beside him, shoving the orange flotation device at him, and telling him to relax, that everything was going to be all right.

But everything was not going to be all right. Even as the lifeguard was speaking, I saw a head bob up beside Michael. Though his wet hair was plastered to his face, I still recognized Josh, the ringleader of the RLS Angels—a ghostly little group so hellbent on mischief making...and evidently worse.

I couldn't speak, of course—my lips, I was sure, were turning blue. But I could still punch. I pulled my arm back and let go of a good one, packed with all the panic I felt at finding myself with nothing but water beneath my feet.

Josh either didn't remember me from Jimmy's or the mall, or didn't recognize me with my hair all wet. In any case, he'd been paying no attention to me at all.

Until my fist connected solidly with his nasal cartilage, that is.

Bone crunched quite satisfyingly under my knuckles, and Josh let out a pain-filled shriek that only I could hear.

Or so I thought. I'd forgotten about the other angels.

At least until I was abruptly pulled under the waves by two sets of hands that had wrapped around my ankles.

Let me just mention something here. While to the rest of humanity, ghosts have no actual matter—most of you walk right through them all the time and don't even know it; maybe you feel a cold spot, or you get a strange chill, like Kelly and Debbie did at the convenience mart—to a mediator, they are most definitely made of flesh and bone. As illustrated by my slamming my fist into Josh's face.

But because they have no matter where humans are concerned, ghosts must resort to more creative methods of harming their intended victims than, say, wrapping their hands around their necks. It was for that reason that Josh was using seaweed instead. He could pick up the seaweed—with an effort, like the beer in the Quick Mart. And he could wrap *that* around Michael's neck. Mission accomplished.

I, on the other hand, being a mediator, was not subject to the laws governing human-ghost contact, and, accordingly, they quickly made use of their unexpected advantage.

Okay, I realized then that I had made a bad mistake. It is one thing to fight bad guys on land, where, I must admit, I am quite resourceful, and—I feel I can say without bragging—quite agile.

But it is quite another thing altogether to try to fight something underwater. Particularly something that does not need to breathe as often as I do. Ghosts do breathe—some habits are hard to break—but they don't need to, and sometimes, if they've been dead long enough, they realize it. The RLS Angels hadn't been dead very long, but they'd died underwater, so you might say they had a head start on their spectral peers.

Given those circumstances, I saw my situation progressing in one of either of two ways: either I was going to give up, let my lungs fill with water, and drown, or I was going to completely freak out, strike at anything that came near me, and make those ghosts sorry they'd ever chosen not to go into the light.

I don't suppose it will come as any big surprise to anyone—with the exception of myself, maybe—that I chose the second option.

The hands that were wrapped around my ankles, I realized—though it took me a while; I was pretty disoriented—were connected to bodies, attached to which, presumably, were heads. There is nothing so unpleasant, I know from experience, as a foot to the face. And so I very promptly, and with all my strength, kicked in the direction that I supposed those faces might be, and was gratified to feel soft facial bones give way beneath my heels.

Then with my arms, which were still free, I gave a mighty stroke, and broke back through the water's surface, gulping in a huge lungful of air—and checking to make sure Michael had gotten well and truly away, which he had; the lifeguard was towing him back to shore—before I dove down again, in search of my attackers.

I found them easily enough. They were still in their prom wear, and the girls' dresses were floating all around them like seaweed. I grabbed a handful of one, tugged it toward me, and saw, in the murky water, the very startled face of Felicia Bruce. Before she had a chance to react, I plunged a thumb into her eye. She screamed, but since we were underwater, I didn't hear a thing. I just saw a trail of bubbles racing for the water's surface.

Then someone grabbed me from behind. I reacted by thrusting my head back, as hard as I could, and was delighted to feel my skull make very hard contact with my attacker's forehead. The hands that had been holding me instantly let go, and I spun around, and saw Mark Pulsford swimming hastily away. Some football player he'd been, if he couldn't take a simple head butt.

I felt the urgent need to breathe, so I followed the last of the bubbles from Felicia's scream, and resurfaced just as the ghosts did, too.

We all bobbed there on the surface: me, Josh, Felicia, Mark, and a very white-faced Carrie.

"Omigod," Carrie said. Her teeth, unlike mine, weren't chattering. "It's that girl. That girl from Jimmy's. I told you she can see us."

Josh, whose broken nose had sprung, cartoonlike, back into place, was nevertheless wary of me.

Even if you happen to be dead, getting your nose broken hurts a lot.

"Hey," he said to me as I treaded water. "This isn't your fight, okay? Stay out of it."

I tried to say, "Oh, yeah? Well, listen up. I'm the mediator, and you guys have a choice. You can go on to your next life with your teeth in or your teeth out. Which is it going to be?"

Only my own teeth were chattering so hard, all that came out was a bunch of weird noises that sounded like, Oah? Esup. Imameator an—

You get the picture.

Since Father Dominic's technique—reasoning—didn't appear to be working in this particular instance, I abandoned it. Instead, I reached out and grabbed the rope of seaweed they'd tried to strangle Michael with and flung it around the necks of the two girls, who were treading water close to each other, and to me. They looked extremely surprised to find themselves lassoed like a couple of seacows.

And I can't really tell you what I was thinking, but it's probably safe to say my plan—though somewhat haphazardly formed—involved towing them both back to shore where I intended to beat the crap out of them.

While the girls clawed at their necks and attempted to escape, the boys came at me. I didn't care. I was furious all of a sudden. They had ruined my nice time at the beach and tried to drown my date. Granted I wasn't particularly fond of Michael, but I certainly didn't want to see him drowned before my eyes—particularly not now that I knew what a hottie he was under his sweater vest.

Holding onto the girls with one hand, I thrust out the other and managed to grab Josh by—what else?—the short hairs on the back of his neck.

Though this proved highly effective—in that he promptly began thrashing in pain—I'd neglected two things. One was Mark, who continued to swim free. And the other was the ocean, which was still churning waves at me. Any sensible person would have been looking out for these things, but I, in my anger, was not.

Which was why a second later, I was promptly sucked under.

Let me tell you, there are probably pleasanter ways to die than choking on a lungful of saltwater. It burns, you know? I mean, it is, after all, *salt*.

And I coughed down a lot of it, thanks first to the wave, which bowled me under. And then I swallowed a lot more when Mark grabbed hold of my ankle, and kept me under.

One thing I have to admit about the ocean: it's very quiet down there. I mean, really. No more shrieking gulls, crashing of the waves, shouts from the surfers. No, under the sea, it's just you and the water and the ghosts who are trying to kill you.

Because, of course, I'd held onto the ends of the seaweed I was using to tow the girls. And I hadn't let go of Josh's hair, either.

I kind of liked it, I discovered, under there. It wasn't so bad, really. Except for the cold, and the salt, and the horrible realization that at any moment, a twenty-foot killer shark could swoop under me and bite my leg off, it was, well, almost pleasant.

I suppose I lost consciousness for a few seconds. I

mean, I'd have had to, to have held onto those stupid ghosts so tightly, and think being held under tons and tons of salt water was pleasant.

The next thing I knew, something was tugging at me, and it wasn't one of the ghosts. I was being tugged *toward* the surface, where I could see the last rays of the sun winking across the waves. I looked up, and was surprised to see a flash of orange and a lot of blond hair. Why, I thought, wonderingly, it's that nice lifeguard. What's he doing here?

And then I became greatly concerned for him, because, of course, there were a lot of bloodthirsty ghosts around, and it was entirely possible one of them might try to hurt him.

But when I looked around, I found, to my astonishment, that all of them had disappeared. I was still holding the rope of seaweed, and my other hand was still clenched as if on someone's hair. But there was nothing there. Just seawater.

The chickens, I thought to myself. The lousy chickens. Came up against the mediator and found out you couldn't take it, huh? Well, let that be a lesson to you! You don't mess with the mediator.

And then I did something that will probably live on in mediator infamy for the rest of time:

I blacked out.

CHAPTER 8

Okay, I don't know if any of you have ever lost consciousness before, so let me just say here real quickly:

Don't do it. Really. If you can avoid situations in which you might lose consciousness, please do so. Whatever else you do, do not pass out. Trust me. It is not fun. It is not fun at all.

Unless, of course, you're guaranteed to wake up having mouth-to-mouth performed on you by a totally hot California lifeguard. Then I say go for it.

That was my experience when I opened my eyes that afternoon on the Carmel Beach. One second I was sucking in lungfuls of saltwater, and the next I was lip-locked with Brad Pitt. Or at least someone who looked very much like him.

Could this, I asked myself, my heart turning over in my chest, be my one true love?

Then the lips left mine, and I saw that it wasn't my true love at all, but the lifeguard, his long blond hair falling wetly around his tanned face. The skin around his blue eyes crinkled with concern—the ravages of sun; he should have used Coppertone—as he asked, "Miss? Miss, can you hear me?"

"Suze," I heard a familiar voice—Gina? but what was Gina doing in California?—say. "Her name is Suze."

"Suze," the lifeguard said, giving my cheeks a couple of rather rough little taps. "Blink if you can understand me."

This, I thought, could not possibly be my one true love. He seems to think I'm a moron. Also, why does he keep hitting me?

"Oh, my God." Cee Cee's voice was more high-pitched than usual. "Is she paralyzed?"

To prove to them I wasn't paralyzed, I started to sit up.

Then promptly realized this had been a bad decision.

I think I only threw up once. To say that I spewed like Mount St. Helens is a gross exaggeration on Dopey's part. It is true that a great deal of seawater came up out of me after I tried to sit up. But fortunately, I avoided throwing it up on both myself and the lifeguard, sending most of it neatly into the sand beside me.

After I was done throwing up, I felt a great deal better.

"Suze!" Gina—who I suddenly remembered was in California visiting me—was on her knees beside me. "Are you all right? I was so worried! You just laid there so still...."

Sleepy was a lot less sympathetic.

"What the hell were you thinking?" he demanded. "Did Pamela Anderson die and leave an opening on the *Baywatch* rescue squad, or something?"

I looked up at all the anxious faces around me. Really, I'd had no idea so many people cared. But there was Gina and Cee Cee and Adam and Dopey and Sleepy and some of their surfer friends and a few tourists, snapping pictures of the real live drowned girl, and Michael and...

Michael. My gaze snapped back toward him. Michael, who was in so much danger, and hardly seemed aware of it. Michael, who, as he stood dripping over me, seemed unconscious of the fact that around his throat was a great red welt where the seaweed had bit into his skin. It looked painfully inflamed.

"I'm all right," I said, and started to stand up.

"No," the lifeguard said. "There's an ambulance on its way. Stay where you are until the dudes from EMS have checked you out."

"Um," I said. "No, thank you."

Then I stood up and moved toward my towel, which still rested where I'd left it beside Gina's, a little farther up the beach.

"Miss," the lifeguard said, hurrying after me. "You were unconscious. You nearly drowned. You've got to be checked out by EMS. It's procedure."

"You really," Cee Cee said as she jogged along beside me, "should let them check you out, Suze. Rick says he thinks both you and Michael might have been victims of a Portuguese man-of-war."

I blinked at her. "Rick? Who's Rick?"

"The lifeguard," Cee Cee said with exasperation.

Apparently, while I'd been unconscious, everyone had gotten to know one another. "That's why he had them hang out the yellow flag."

I squinted and peered up at the flag that now fluttered from the top of the lifeguard's chair. Usually green, except when riptides or extreme undertows were reported, it flew bright yellow, urging beachgoers to use caution in the water.

"I mean, look at Michael's neck," Cee Cee continued. I looked obligingly at Michael's neck.

"Rick says when he got there, there was something around my neck," Michael said. He couldn't, I noticed, seem to meet my gaze. "He thought it was a giant squid, at first. But that couldn't be, of course. There's never been one spotted this far north before. So he thought it must have been a man-of-war."

I didn't say anything. I was quite certain that Rick really did believe that Michael had been the victim of a Portuguese man-of-war. The human mind will do whatever it must to trick itself into believing anything but the truth—that there might be something else out there, something unexplainable...something not quite normal.

Something *para*normal.

So the rope of seaweed that had been wrapped around Michael's throat became the arm of a giant squid, and then, later, the stinging tentacle of a jellyfish. It certainly couldn't have been what it had appeared to be: a piece of seaweed being used with deadly intent by a pair of invisible hands.

"And look at your ankles," Cee Cee said.

I looked down. Around both my ankles were

bright red marks, like rope burns. Only they weren't rope burns. They were the places Felicia and Carrie had grabbed me, trying to drag me down to the ocean floor, and to certain death.

Those stupid girls needed manicures, and badly.

"You're lucky," Adam said. "I've been stung by a man-of-war before, and it hurts like a—"

His voice trailed off as he noticed Gina listening intently. Gina, who had four brothers, had certainly heard every swear word in the book, but Adam was much too gentlemanly to utter any in front of her.

"A lot," he finished up. "But you guys don't seem to have been hurt too badly. Well, except for that whole drowning thing."

I reached for my towel, and did my best to wipe off the sand that seemed to be coating me all over. What had that lifeguard done, anyway? Dragged me through the stuff?

"Well," I said. "I'm okay now. No harm done."

Sleepy, who'd followed me over along with everybody else, went, exasperatedly, "It is not okay, Suze. Do what the lifeguard tells you. Don't make me have to call Mom and Dad."

I looked at him in surprise. Not because I was mad about his threatening to rat me out, but because he'd called my mother *Mom*. He'd never done it before. My stepbrothers' own mother had died years and years ago.

Well, I thought to myself. She *is* the best mother in the world.

"Go ahead and call them," I said. "I don't care."

I saw Sleepy and the lifeguard exchange meaningful looks. I hurried to find my clothes, and started to wiggle into them, pulling them on right over my damp bikini. I wasn't trying to be difficult. Really, I wasn't. It's just that I totally could not afford a trip to the hospital just then, and the three-hour wait it would entail. In those three hours, I was fairly certain the RLS Angels were going launch another attack against Michael...and I could not in good conscience leave him to their devices.

"I am not," Sleepy said, folding his arms across his chest, a motion that caused the rubber of the wet-suit he was still wearing to squeak audibly, "taking you home unless you let the EMS guys check you out first."

I turned toward Michael, who looked extremely surprised when I asked him, politely, "Michael, would *you* mind taking me home?"

Now he seemed to have no problem meeting my gaze. His eyes very wide behind his glasses—he'd evidently found them where I'd abandoned them on my towel—he stammered, "Of c-course!"

This caused the lifeguard to shake his head in disgust and stomp away. Everyone else just stood around looking at me as if I were demented. Gina was the only one who came up to me as I was gathering up my books and preparing to follow Michael to where his car was parked.

"You and I," she whispered, "are going to be doing some talking when you get home."

I regarded her with what I hoped was an innocent look. The last slanting rays of the sun had set her aura of copper-colored curls glowing like a flaming halo.

"What do you mean?" I asked.

"You *know* what I mean," she said meaningfully.

And then she turned around and sauntered back over to where Sleepy stood, regarding me worriedly.

The truth was, I *did* know what she meant. She meant Michael. What was I doing, messing around with a boy like Michael, who was so obviously not my one true love?

But the thing was, I couldn't tell her. I couldn't tell her that Michael was being stalked by four ghosts with murderous intent, and that it was my sacred duty as a mediator to protect him.

Although considering what happened later on that night, I probably should have.

"So," I said, as soon as Michael got the car—his mother's minivan again; his car, he explained, was still in the shop—going. "We need to talk."

Michael, now that he was back in his glasses and clothes, wasn't nearly the intimidatingly buff male specimen he'd been without them. Like Superman when he was in his Clark Kent attire, Michael had turned back into a stammering geek.

Only I couldn't help noticing, as he stammered, how nicely he filled out that sweater vest.

"Talk?" He gripped the wheel quite tightly as we sat in what, for Carmel, represented rush-hour traffic: a single tour bus and a Volkswagen filled with surfboards. "W-what about?"

"About what happened to you this weekend."

Michael turned his head sharply to look at me, then just as quickly turned back to face the road. "W-what do you m-mean?" he asked.

"Come off it, Michael," I said. I figured there was no point in being gentle with him. It was like a Band-

Aid that needed to come off: either you did it with agonizing slowness, or you got it over with, hard and quick. "I know about the accident."

The tour bus finally started moving. Michael put his foot on the gas.

"Well," he said after a minute, a wry smile on his face, though he kept his eyes on the road, "you must not blame me too much, or you wouldn't have asked for a ride."

"Blame you for what?" I asked him.

"Four people died in that accident." Michael picked up a half-empty can of Coke from the cup holder between our seats. "And I'm still alive." He took a quick swallow and put the can back. "You be the judge."

I didn't like his tone. It wasn't that it was self-pitying. It was that it wasn't. He sounded hostile. And he wasn't stammering anymore, I noticed.

"Well," I said carefully. Like I mentioned, Father Dominic is the one who's good at reasoning. I'm more like the muscle of our little mediator family. I knew I was venturing out into deep and troubled waters—if you'll excuse the pun.

"I read in the paper today that your breath test came back negative for alcohol," I said cautiously.

"So?" Michael exploded, startling me a little. "What does that prove?"

I blinked at him. "Well, that you, at least, weren't drinking and driving."

He seemed to relax a little. He said, "Oh." Then he asked, tentatively, "Do you want…"

I looked at him. We were driving along the coastline, and the sun, sinking into the water, had cast everything into either brilliant orange or deep shadow. The light reflecting off the lenses of Michael's glasses made it impossible to read his expression.

"Do you want to see where it happened?" he asked all in a rush, as if he wanted to get the words out before he changed his mind.

"Um, sure," I said. "If you feel like you want to show me."

"I do." He turned his head to look at me, but once again, I couldn't read his eyes behind his glasses. "If you don't mind. It's weird, but...I really feel like you might understand."

Ha! I thought smugly to myself. Take that, Father Dom! All your nagging about how I always hit first and talk later. Well, look at me now!

"Why did you do it?" Michael asked abruptly, interrupting my self-congratulations.

I threw a startled glance in his direction. "Do what?" I genuinely hadn't the slightest idea what he was talking about.

"Go in," he said in that same quiet voice, "after me."

"Oh." I cleared my throat. "That. Well, you see, Michael..."

"Never mind."

When I glanced over at him, I saw he was smiling.

"Don't worry about it," he said. "You don't have to tell me. I know." His voice dropped about an octave. I looked over at him in alarm. "I know."

And then he reached across the Coke can, nestled in the cup holder between our seats, and dropped his right hand over my left.

Oh, my God! I felt my stomach lurch all over again, just like it had back down at the beach.

Because suddenly it was all very clear to me. Michael Meducci didn't just have a crush on me. Oh, no. It was much, much worse than that:

Michael Meducci thinks *I* have a crush on *him*.

Michael Meducci thinks I *more* than just have a crush on him. Michael Meducci thinks I'm in love with him.

I had just one thing to say, and since I couldn't say it out loud, I said it in my head:

EEEEW!

I mean, he might have looked good in a bathing suit and all, but Michael Meducci still wasn't exactly...

Well, Jesse.

And that, I thought with a sigh, is pretty much how my love life is going to go from now on, isn't it?

CHAPTER

9

Carefully, I tried to pull my hand out from under Michael's.

"Oh," he said, lifting his hand off mine so he could grip the wheel. "It's coming up. Where the accident happened, I mean."

Hideously relieved, I glanced to my right. We were moving along Highway 1 at quite a little clip. The sands of Carmel Beach had turned into the majestic cliffs of Big Sur. A few more miles down the coast, and we'd hit redwood groves and Point Sur Lighthouse. Big Sur was a haven for hikers and campers, and just about anybody who liked magnificent views and breathtaking natural beauty. Me, I'll take the views, but nature leaves me cold...especially after a little poison oak incident that had occurred a week or two after I'd arrived in California.

And don't even get me started on ticks.

Big Sur—or at least the pretty much one-lane road that winds along it—also hosts quite a few hairpin curves. Michael eased around a completely blind one just as a Winnebago, coming from the other direction, came thundering around the other side of this massive cliff. There wasn't exactly room for both vehicles, and considering that all that was separating us from the sheer drop-off to the sea was a metal guardrail, it was a bit disconcerting. Michael, however, backed up—we hadn't been going that fast—and then pulled over, allowing the Winnebago to ease by with only a foot or so of room to spare.

"Jeez," I said, glancing back at the huge RV. "That's kind of dangerous, huh?"

Michael shrugged. "You're supposed to honk," he said, "as you round that corner. To let anyone behind that rock thing know you're there. That guy didn't know, obviously, because he's a tourist." Michael cleared his throat. "That's what happened, um, on Saturday night."

I sat up straighter in my seat.

"This—" I swallowed. "—is where it happened?"

"Yeah," Michael said. There was no change in the inflection of his voice at all. "This is it."

And indeed it was. Now that I knew to look for them, I could plainly see the black skid marks the wheels of Josh's car had left as he'd tried to keep from going over. A large section of the guardrail had already been replaced, the metal shiny and new just where the skid marks ended.

I asked, in a quiet voice, "Can we stop?"

"Sure," Michael said.

There was a scenic overlook around the corner, not a hundred yards away from where the cars had narrowly missed each other. Michael pulled into it and turned off the engine.

"Observation point," he said, pointing to the wooden sign in front of us that said, *Observation point. No Littering.* "A lot of kids come here on Saturday night." Michael cleared his throat and looked at me meaningfully. "And park."

I have to say, up until that moment I really had no idea I was capable of moving as fast as I did getting out of that car. But I was unbuckled and out of that seat quicker than you could say *ectoplasm.*

The sun had almost completely set now, and it was already growing chilly. I hugged myself as I stood on tiptoe to look over the edge of the cliff, my hair whipping my face in the wind off the sea, which was much wilder and cooler up here than it had been back down on the beach. The rhythmic pulse of the sea below us was loud, much louder than the engines of the cars going by on Highway 1.

There were, I noticed, no gulls. No birds of any kind.

That should, of course, have been my first clue. But as usual, I missed it.

Instead, all I could concentrate on was how sheer the drop was. Hundreds of feet, straight down, into waves churning against giant boulders knocked down from the cliffsides during various earthquakes. Not exactly the kind of cliff you'd catch anyone—not even Elvis back in his Acapulco prime—diving off.

Strangely, at the bottom of the place where Josh's car had gone off of the road was a small, sandy beach. Not the kind you'd go to sunbathe, but a nice picnic area, if you were willing to risk your neck climbing down to get there.

Michael must have noticed my gaze, since he said, "Yeah, that's where they landed. Not in the water. Well, at least, not right away. Then high tide came in, and—"

I shuddered and looked away.

"Is there some way," I wondered aloud, "to get down there?"

"Sure," he said, and pointed at an open section of the guardrail. "Over there. It's a trail. Hikers are the only ones who use it, mostly. But sometimes tourists try it. The beach down there is amazing. You never saw such huge waves. Only it's too dangerous to surf. Too many riptides."

I looked at him curiously in the purpling twilight. "You've been down there?" I asked. The surprise in my voice must have been evident.

"Suze," he said with a smile. "I've lived here all my life. There aren't a whole lot of beaches I haven't been to."

I nodded, and pulled at a strand of hair that had found its way into my mouth thanks to the wind. "So, what," I asked him, "happened, exactly, that night?"

He squinted at the road. It was dark enough now that the cars traveling on it had switched on their lights. Occasionally, the glow of one swept his face as he spoke. Again, it was difficult to see his eyes behind the reflection of the light against the lenses of his glasses.

"I was coming home," he said, "from a workshop at Esalen—"

"Esalen?"

"Yeah. The Esalen Institute. You've never heard of it?" He shook his head. "My God, I thought it was known worldwide." My expression must have been pretty blank, since he said, "Well, anyway, I was at a lecture there. 'Colonization of Other Worlds, and What It Means for Exterrestrials Here on Earth.' "

I tried not to burst out laughing. I was, after all, a girl who could see and speak to ghosts. Who was I to say there wasn't life on other planets?

"Anyway, I was driving home—it was pretty late, I guess—and they came barreling around that corner, didn't honk, nothing."

I nodded. "So what did you do?"

"Well, I swerved to avoid them, of course, and ended up going into that cliff there. You can't see it because it's dark out now, but my front bumper took out a big chunk of the side of the hill. And they...well, they swerved the other way, and it was foggy, and the road might have been a little slick, and they were going really fast, and..."

He finished, tonelessly, with another shrug. "And they went over."

I shuddered again. I couldn't help it. I had met these kids, remember. They hadn't exactly been at their best—in fact, they'd been trying to kill me—but still, I couldn't help feeling sorry for them. It was a long, long way down.

"So what did you do?" I asked.

"Me?" He seemed strangely surprised by the question. "Well, I hit my head, you know, so I blacked out. I didn't come around until someone pulled over and checked on me. That's when I asked what happened to the other car. And they said 'What other car?' And I thought they'd, you know, driven away, and I have to admit, I was pretty hacked. I mean, that they hadn't bothered to call an ambulance for me, or anything. But then we saw the guard-rail...."

I was getting really cold now. The sun was completely gone, although the western sky was still streaked violet and red. I shivered and said, "Let's get in the car."

And so we did.

We sat there staring at the horizon as it turned a deeper and deeper shade of blue. The headlights from the cars that went by occasionally lit up the interior of the minivan. Inside the car it was much quieter, without the wind and the sound of the waves below us. Another wave of extreme tiredness passed over me. I could see by the glow of the clock in the dashboard that soon it would be dinnertime. My stepfather Andy had a very strict rule about dinner. You showed up. Period.

"Look," I said, breaking the stillness. "It sounds horrible, what happened. But it wasn't your fault."

He looked at me. In the green glow from the instruments in the dash, I could see that his smile was rueful. "Wasn't it?" he asked.

"No," I said sternly. "It was an accident, plain and simple. The problem is...well, not everyone sees it that way."

The smile disappeared. "Who doesn't see it that way?" he demanded. "The cops? I gave them my statement. They seemed satisfied. They took a blood sample. I tested completely negative for alcohol, for all drugs. They can't possibly—"

"Not," I said quickly, "the cops." How, I wondered, was I going to put this? I mean, the guy was obviously one of those UFO geeks, so you'd think he wouldn't have a problem with ghosts, but you never knew.

"The thing is," I began, carefully, "I've kind of noticed that since the accident this weekend, you've been a bit...danger prone."

"Yeah," Michael said. All of a sudden, his hand was on mine again. "If it wasn't for you, I might even be dead. That's twice now you've saved my life."

"Ha ha," I said nervously, pulling my hand away, and pretending I had another hair in my mouth so I needed to use that particular hand, you know, to brush it away. "Um, but seriously, haven't you kind of, I mean, wondered what was going on? Like why all of a sudden so many...*things* were happening to you?"

He smiled at me again. His teeth, in the glow of the speedometer, looked green. "It must be fate," he said.

"Okay," I said. *Why me?* "Not those kind of things. I mean *bad* kind of things. Like at the mall. And at the beach just now...."

"Oh," he said. Then he shrugged those incredibly strong shoulders. "No."

"Okay," I said yet again. "But if you were to think about it, don't you think one sort of logical explanation might be...angry spirits?"

His smile faded a little. "What do you mean?"

I heaved a sigh. "Look, that wasn't a jellyfish back there, and you know it. You were being pulled under, Michael. By something."

He nodded. "I know. I haven't quite...I'm used to undertows, of course, but that was—"

"It wasn't an undertow. And it wasn't jellyfish. And I just...well, I think you should be careful."

"What are you saying?" Michael asked. He peered at me curiously. "It almost sounds like you're suggesting that I've been the victim of some kind of...demonic force." He laughed. In the quiet of the car, his laugh was loud. "Brought on by the deaths of those kids who almost ran me off of the road? Is that it?"

I looked out my window. I couldn't see anything except the huge purple shadows of the steep cliffs around us, but I kept looking anyway. "Yes," I said. "That's exactly it."

"Suze." Michael reached for my hand again, and this time, he squeezed it. "Are you trying to tell me that you believe in ghosts?"

I looked at him. I looked him straight in the eye. And I said, "Yes, Michael. Yes, I am."

He laughed again. "Oh, come on," he said. "Do you honestly think that *Josh Saunders* and his friends are capable of communicating from beyond the grave?"

Something in the way he said Josh's name caused me to...I don't know. But I didn't like it. I didn't like it at all.

"I mean—" Michael let go of my hand, then leaned forward and switched on the ignition. "Face facts. The guy was a dumb jock. The most impressive thing he ever did was plunge off of a cliff with another dumb jock, and their equally low-wattage girlfriends. It's not necessarily such a bad thing they're gone, you know? They were just taking up space."

My jaw sagged. I felt it. And yet there didn't seem to be anything I could do about it.

"And as for any of them being able to summon up any sort of powers of darkness," Michael said, putting vocal quotes around the words *powers of darkness,* "to avenge their pitifully stupid deaths, well, thanks for the warning, but I think that whole *I Know What You Did Last Summer* thing has pretty much been played out, don't you?"

I stared at him. Really stared at him. I couldn't believe it. So much for Mr. Sensitive. I guess he only stammered and blushed when his own life was being threatened. He didn't seem to care very much about anybody else's.

Unless maybe he was going out with them on Friday night, as was illustrated by his comment as we were about to pull out onto the highway again:

"Hey," he said with a wink. "Buckle up."

CHAPTER 10

I flung myself into my seat just as everybody else was picking up their forks.

Ha! Not late! Not technically, since no one had actually started eating yet.

"And where have you been, Suze?" my mother asked, lifting a basket of rolls and passing it directly to Gina. Good thing, too. Otherwise, given the way my brothers ate, that thing would be empty before it ever reached her.

"I went," I said as Max, my stepbrothers' extremely large, extremely slobbery dog, dropped his head down upon my lap, his traditional station at mealtimes, and rolled his soft brown eyes up at me, "on a drive."

"With whom?" my mother asked in that same mild tone, the one that indicated that if I didn't answer carefully, I could potentially be in serious trouble.

Before I could say anything, Dopey went, "Michael Meducci," and made some gagging noises.

Andy raised his eyebrows. "That boy who was here last night?"

"That'd be the one," I said, shooting Dopey a dirty look that he ignored. Gina and Sleepy, I noticed, had taken care to sit beside each other and were strangely quiet. I wondered, if I dropped my napkin and leaned down to pick it up, what I'd see going on underneath the table. Probably, I thought to myself, something I did not particularly care to see. I kept my napkin tightly in my lap.

"Meducci," my mother murmured. "Why is that name familiar to me?"

"Doubtlessly," Doc said, "you are thinking of the Medicis, an Italian noble family that produced three popes and two queens of France. Cosimo the Elder was the first to rule Florence, while Lorenzo the Magnificent was a patron of the arts, with clients that included Michelangelo and Botticelli."

My mother looked at him curiously. "Actually," she said, "that's not what I was thinking."

I knew what was coming. My mom has a memory like a steel trap. She needs it, of course, in her line of work. But I knew it was only a matter of time before she figured out where she'd heard Michael's name before.

"He was the one who was in that accident this weekend," I said, to hasten the inevitable. "The one where those four RLS students were killed."

Dopey dropped his fork. It made quite a clatter as it landed on his plate.

"Michael *Meducci?*" He shook his head. "No way. That was *Michael Meducci?* You are shitting me."

Andy said, sharply, "Brad. Language, please."

Dopey said, "Sorry," but his eyes, I noticed, were very bright. "Michael Meducci," he said again. "Michael Meducci killed Mark Pulsford?"

"He didn't kill anybody," I snapped. I could see I should have kept my mouth shut. Now it was going to be all over school. "It was an accident."

"Really, Brad," Andy said. "I'm sure the poor boy didn't mean to kill anyone."

"Well, I'm sorry," Dopey said. "But Mark Pulsford was like one of the best quarterbacks in the state. Seriously. He had a scholarship to UCLA, the whole thing. That guy was really cool."

"Oh, yeah? Then what was he doing hanging around you?" Sleepy, in a rare moment of wit, grinned at his brother.

"Shut up," Dopey said. "We happen to have partied together."

"Right," Sleepy said with a sneer.

"We did," Dopey insisted. "Last month, in the Valley. Mark was the bomb." He grabbed a roll, stuffed most of it into his mouth, then said around the doughy mass, "Until Michael Meducci came along and murdered him, that is."

I noticed that Gina was observing me with one eyebrow—one only—raised. I ignored her.

"The accident wasn't Michael's fault," I said. "At least, he hasn't been charged with anything."

My mother laid down her own fork. "The investigation into the accident," she said, "is still ongoing."

"As many accidents as they've had," my stepfather said as he rolled a few spears of asparagus onto my mother's plate, then passed the platter of them to Gina, "on that section of highway, you would think somebody would do something to improve the road conditions."

"The narrow stretch of highway," Doc said conversationally, "along the one-hundred-mile stretch of seacoast known as Big Sur has traditionally been considered treacherous—even highly dangerous. Frequently enshrouded with coastal fog, this winding and narrow mountainous road is, thanks to historical preservationists, unlikely to be expanded. The very isolation of the area is what has held such appeal for the many poets and artists who have made their homes there, including Robinson Jeffers, who found the splendor of the bleak wilderness highly appealing."

I blinked at my youngest stepbrother. His photographic memory could, at times, be annoying, but for the most part it was highly useful, particularly when term paper time came rolling around.

"Thanks," I said, "for that."

Doc smiled, revealing a mouthful of food-encrusted braces. "Don't mention it."

"The worst part of it," Andy said, continuing his rant on the safety conditions on Highway 1, "is that young drivers seem irresistibly drawn to that particular stretch of road."

Dopey, shoveling wild rice into his mouth as if it were the first food he'd seen in weeks, snickered and said, "Well, duh, Dad."

Andy looked at his middle-born son. "You know, Brad," he said mildly. "In America—and, I'm told, much of Europe—it is considered socially acceptable to occasionally lay down our fork between bites, and spend some time actually chewing."

"That's where the action is," Dopey said, laying down his fork as his father had suggested, but compensating by speaking with his mouth full.

"What action?" my stepfather asked curiously.

Sleepy, who generally didn't speak unless absolutely forced to, had grown almost garrulous since Gina's arrival. "He means the Point," Sleepy said.

My mother looked confused. "The point?"

"The Point," Sleepy corrected her. "The observation point. It's where everybody goes to make out on Saturday night. At least"—Sleepy chuckled to himself—"Brad and his friends."

Dopey, far from taking offense at this slanderous remark, waved an asparagus spear as if it were a cigar while he explained, "The Point is the bomb."

"Is that," Doc asked interestedly, "where you take Debbie Mancuso?" and then he winced in pain as one of his shins was brutally assaulted beneath the table. "Ow!"

"Debbie Mancuso and I are not going out!" Dopey bellowed.

"Brad," Andy said. "Do not kick your brother. David, do not invoke Miss Mancuso's name at the dinner table. We've talked about this. And Suze?"

I looked up with raised eyebrows.

"I don't like the idea of you getting into a car with a boy who was involved in a fatal accident, whether it was his fault or not." Andy looked at my mother. "Do you agree?"

"I'm afraid I'm going to have to," my mother said. "I feel bad about it. The Meduccis have certainly been through some trying times lately—" When my stepfather looked at her questioningly, my mother said, "Their little girl was the one who almost drowned a few weeks ago. You remember."

"Oh." Andy nodded. "At that pool party. There was no parental supervision—"

"And plenty of alcohol," my mother said. "Poor thing apparently drank too much and fell in. Nobody noticed—or if they did, nobody did anything about it. Not until it was too late. She's been in a coma ever since. If she lives, it will be with severe brain damage. Suze." My mother laid down her fork. "I don't think it's a good idea for you to be seeing this boy."

Ordinarily, this would have cheered me up considerably. I mean, I wasn't exactly looking forward to going out with the guy.

But I sort of had to. I mean, if I was to have any hope at all of keeping him from slipping into a nerd coffin.

"Why?" I carefully swallowed a mouthful of salmon. "It's not Michael's fault his sister's an alcoholic who can't swim. And what were her parents thinking, anyway, letting an eighth grader go to a party like that?"

"That," my mother said, her mouth tightening, "is not the issue here, and you know it. You're just going to have to call that young man and tell him that your mother absolutely forbids you to get into a vehicle with him. If he wants to come here and spend the evening with you watching videos or whatever, that's fine. But you are not getting into a car with him."

My eyes widened. *Here?* Spend the evening *here?* Under Jesse's watchful eye? Oh, God, just what I needed. The image these words conveyed filled me with such horror, the forkful of salmon I'd had poised before my lips fell into my lap, where it was instantly vacuumed up by a long canine tongue.

My mother touched my hand. "Suze," she said softly. "I really mean it. I don't want you getting into a car with that boy."

I looked at my mother curiously. It's true that in times past I have been forced to disobey her, largely due to circumstances beyond my control. But she didn't know that. That I had disobeyed her, I mean. For the most part, I'd managed to keep my transgressions to myself—except for the occasions I'd been brought home by the police, incidents so few they are hardly worth mentioning.

But since that had not been the case in this situation, I didn't quite understand why she felt it necessary to repeat her edict concerning Michael Meducci.

"Okay, Mom," I said. "I got it the first time."

"It's just something I feel very strongly about," she said.

I looked at her. It wasn't that she appeared...well, guilty. But she definitely knew something. Something she wasn't letting on.

This was not particularly surprising. A television journalist, my mother was often privy to information not necessarily meant for release to the public. She wasn't one of those reporters you hear about, either, who'd do anything to get the "big" story. If a cop told my mother something—and they often do; my mother, even though she's forty-something, is still pretty hot, and just about anybody would tell her anything she wanted to know if she licked her lips enough—he could depend on her not mentioning it on air if he asked her not to. That's just how she is.

I wondered what, exactly, she knew about Michael Meducci and the accident that had killed the four Angels.

Enough, apparently, to keep her from wanting me to hang around with him.

I didn't exactly think she was being particularly unfair to him, either. I couldn't help remembering what Michael had said in the car, right before pulling back out onto the highway: *They were just taking up space.*

Suddenly, I didn't blame those kids so much for trying to drown him.

"Okay, Mom," I said. "I get it."

Apparently satisfied, my mother turned back to her salmon, which Andy had grilled to perfection and served with a delicate dill sauce.

"So how are you going to break it to him?" Gina asked a half hour later as she helped me load the dishwasher after dinner—having brushed aside my mother's insistence that, as a guest, she did not have to do this.

"I don't know," I said hesitantly. "You know, the whole Clark Kent thing aside—"

"Geeky on the outside, dreamy in the middle?"

"Yeah. In spite of that—which is hard to resist, believe me—he's still kind of got this quality that strikes me as..."

"Stalkery?" Gina said, rinsing the salad bowl before handing it to me to put in the dishwasher rack.

"Maybe that's it. I don't know."

"It was very stalkery how he showed up here last

night," she said. "Without even calling first. Any guy ever tried to do that to me"—she waved her fingers in the air and then snapped them—"and he is so gone."

I shrugged. It was different back east, of course. In the city, you simply do not stop by someone's place without calling first. In California, I'd noticed, "drive-bys" were more socially acceptable.

"But don't even act," Gina went on, "like you care, Simon. You don't like that guy. I don't know what, exactly, you've got going on with him, but it definitely isn't anything gonadal."

I thought, fleetingly, of how pleasantly surprised we'd all been when Michael had taken his shirt off. "It might have been," I said with a sigh.

"Please." Gina handed me a fistful of silverware. "You and Supergeek? No. Now, tell me. What is going on with you and this guy?"

I looked down at the silverware I'd been shoving into the dishwasher. "I don't know," I said. I couldn't tell her the truth, of course. "There's just...I've got this feeling that there's more to this accident thing than he's letting on. My mom seems to know something about it. Did you notice?"

"I noticed," Gina said, not really grimly, but not happily, either.

"Well, so...I just can't help wondering what really happened. The night of the wreck. Because... well, that wasn't a jellyfish this afternoon, you know."

Gina just nodded. "I didn't think so. I suppose this all has something to do with that mediator thing, huh?"

"Sort of," I said uncomfortably.

"Right. Which might also explain that little mishap with the fingernail polish the other night?"

I couldn't say anything. I just kept thrusting the silverware into the plastic compartments in the dishwasher door. Forks, spoons, knives.

"All right." Gina turned off the water in the sink and dried her hands on a dishtowel. "What do you want me to do?"

I blinked at her. "Do? You? Nothing."

"Come on. I know you, Simon. You didn't miss homeroom seventy-nine times last year because you were enjoying a leisurely breakfast over at the Mickey D's. I know perfectly well you were out there fighting the undead, making this world a safer place for children, and all that. So what do you want me to do? Cover for you?"

I bit my lip. "Well," I said hesitantly.

"Look, don't worry about me. Jake said he'd take me on his delivery run—which holds a certain appeal, if you can stand getting down and dirty in a car full of pepperoni and pineapple pizzas. But if you want, I can stay here and hang with Brad. He's invited me to a video screening of his favorite movie of all time."

I sucked in my breath. "Not *Hellraiser III...?*"

"Indeed."

Gratitude washed over me like one of those waves that had knocked me senseless. "You would do that for me?"

"For you, Simon, anything. So what's it going to be?"

"Okay." I threw down the dishtowel I'd been

holding. "If you would just stay here and pretend like I'm upstairs in my room with cramps, I will worship you forever. They don't ask questions about cramps. Say that I'm in the bathtub, and then maybe a little while later, say I went to bed early. If anyone calls, will you take it for me?"

"As you wish, Queen Midol."

"Oh, Gina." I grabbed her by the shoulders and gave her a little shake. "You are the best. You understand? The *best*. Don't throw yourself away on my stepbrothers: you could do so much better."

"You just don't see it," Gina said, shaking her head wonderingly. "Your stepbrothers are *hot*. Well, except for that little red-headed one. And hey—" This she added as I was headed to the phone to make a call to Father Dominic. "—I expect compensation, you know."

I blinked at her. "You know I only get twenty bucks a week allowance, but you can have it—"

Gina made a face. "I don't want your money. But a thorough explanation would be nice. You never would give me one. You always just dodged the question. But this time, you owe me." She narrowed her eyes. "I mean, I am going to sit through a screening of *Hellraiser III* for you. You owe me *big* time. And yes," she added, before I could open my mouth, "I won't tell anybody. I promise not to call the *Enquirer* or *Ripley's Believe It or Not.*"

I said, with what dignity I could muster, "I wouldn't have thought otherwise."

Then I picked up the phone and dialed.

CHAPTER

11

"So what is it, exactly," I said as I swung the flashlight back and forth across the sandy trail, "that I'm supposed to be looking for?"

"I'm not sure," Father Dominic, a few steps ahead of me, said. "You'll know, I expect, when you find it."

"Great," I muttered.

It was no joke trying to climb down a mountainside in the dark. If I had known this was what Father Dom was going to suggest when I called, I probably would have put off phoning him. I probably would have just stayed home and watched *Hellraiser III* instead. Or at least attempted to finish my geometry homework. I mean, really. I had already nearly died once that day. The Pythagorean theorem hardly seemed threatening in comparison.

"Don't worry," I heard a guy's voice behind me, laced with tolerant amusement, say. "There's no poison oak."

I turned my head and gave Jesse a very sarcastic

look, even though I doubted he could see it. The moon—if there was one—was hidden behind a thick wall of clouds. Tendrils of fog crept along the cliffside we were climbing down, gathering thickly in the dips the trail made, swirling whenever I set my foot down in it, as if it were recoiling at the prospect of touching me. I tried not to think about movies I'd seen in which horrible things happened to people out in such heavy fog. You know the movies I'm talking about.

At the same time, I tried not to think about all the poison oak that might be brushing up against me. Jesse had been joking, of course, but in his usual way, he had read my mind: I have a real thing about disfiguring skin rashes.

And don't even get me started about snakes, which I had every reason to believe might be curled up all along this sorry excuse for a path, just waiting to take a chunk out of the soft fleshy part of my calf just above my Timberlands.

"Yes," I heard Father Dom say. The fog had rushed in and swallowed him up, and I could see only the faint pinprick of yellow his flashlight made in front of me. "Yes, I can see that the police have already been here. This must be where a section of the guardrail fell. You can see its imprint in the broken weeds."

I staggered blindly along, using the beam from my flashlight primarily to hunt for snakes, but also to make sure I didn't step off the trail and plunge the several hundred feet or so into the churning surf below. Jesse had already reached out twice to steer me gently away from the edge of the path when I'd strayed from it while eyeing a suspicious branch.

Now I nearly staggered off it after colliding hard with Father Dom, who'd stopped in the middle of the trail and crouched down. I hadn't seen him at all, and both he and Jesse had to reach out and grab various articles of my clothing in order to right me again. This was not a little embarrassing.

"Sorry," I muttered, mortified at my own clumsiness. "Um, what are you doing, Father D?"

Father Dominic smiled in that infuriatingly patient way of his, and said, "Examining some of the evidence from the accident. You mentioned that your mother seemed to know something about it, and I have a feeling that I know what."

I zipped my windbreaker up more fully, so that my neck was no longer exposed to the chilly night air. It may have been springtime in California, but it couldn't have been more than forty degrees out there on that cliff. Fortunately, I had brought along gloves—mainly as protection, it must be admitted, from potential contact with poison oak—but they were doing double duty now, keeping my fingers from freezing.

"What do you mean?" I hadn't thought to bring along a hat, and so my ears felt like icicles, and my hair kept whipping around in the cold wind off the sea and smacking me in the eyes.

"Look at this." Father Dominic shined his flashlight along a section of the earth, about six feet long, where the dirt was churned up, and the grass broken. "This, I think, is where the guardrail ended up. But do you notice anything odd about it?"

I pulled some hair out of my mouth and kept my eyes peeled for snakes. "No."

"That particular section of rail seems to have come down in one piece. A vehicle would have to be moving at considerable speed to break through such strong metal fencing, but the fact that the entire section seems to have given way suggests that the metal rivets holding it in place must have snapped."

"Or they were loosened," Jesse suggested quietly.

I blinked up at him. Being dead, Jesse wasn't suffering half as much discomfort as I was. The cold didn't affect him, although the wind was catching on his shirt quite a bit, pulling it out and affording me glimpses of his chest, which, I probably don't need to add, was every bit as buff as Michael's, only not quite as pale.

"Loosened?" For the second time that day, my teeth had started to chatter. "What would cause something like that? Rust?"

"I was thinking something a little more man-made, actually," Jesse said quietly.

I looked from the priest to the ghost, then back again. Father Dominic looked as perplexed as I felt. Jesse had not exactly been invited along on this little expedition, but he had shown up as I'd made my way down the driveway to the spot where Father D had said he'd pick me up. Father Dominic's reaction to the news I'd imparted—about the attempt on Michael's life at the beach, and his odd comments in the car later—had been swift and immediate. We needed, he declared, to find the RLS Angels, and fast.

And the easiest way to do that, of course, was to visit the place where their lives had been lost, a locale, Jesse pointed out, best not visited alone at night by a sixty-year-old priest and a sixteen-year-old girl.

I have no idea what Jesse thought he was protecting us from by coming along: bears? But there he was, and apparently, he had a way better idea than I did about what was going on.

"What do you mean, man-made?" I demanded. "What are you talking about?"

"I just think it's strange," Jesse said, "that a whole section of this railing would give way like that, while the rest—as we saw when we inspected it a little while ago—didn't even bend upon the impact."

Father Dominic blinked. "You're suggesting that someone might have loosened the rivets in anticipation of a vehicle striking it. Is that it, Jesse?"

Jesse nodded. I got what he was driving at, but only after a minute or so.

"Wait a minute," I said. "Are you saying you think *Michael* purposely loosened that section of guardrail so that he could run Josh and the others over the cliff?"

"Someone certainly did," Jesse said. "It might well have been your Michael."

I took umbrage at that. Not at the suggestion that Michael might have done something so heinous, but at Jesse calling him *my* Michael.

"Wait just a minute—" I began. But Father Dominic rather uncharacteristically interrupted me.

"I have to agree with Susannah, Jesse," Father Dominic said. "Certainly it appears that the rail did not perform the function it was intended to. In fact, a rather serious flaw in its design seems to have occurred. But to suggest that someone might have purposefully tampered with it..."

"Susannah," Jesse said. "Didn't you say that

Michael seems to dislike the people who died in the accident?"

"Well," I said, "he did tell me he thought that they were a waste of space. But honestly, Jesse, in order for what you're suggesting to work, Michael would have had to know Josh and those guys were coming. How could he have known that? And he'd have had to wait for them, and then when they started to round the corner, he'd have had to purposefully put down the gas..."

"Well," Jesse said with a shrug. "Yes."

"Impossible." Father Dominic straightened up, brushing dirt from the knees of his trousers. "I refuse even to consider such a possibility. That boy, a cold-blooded murderer? You don't know what you're saying, Jesse. Why, he's got the highest GPA in school. He's a member of the Chess Club."

I patted Father Dominic on the shoulder. "Hate to break it to you, Father D," I said, "but chess players can kill people, just like anyone else." Then I looked down at the gouge mark in the earth where the guardrail had lain. "The real question is why?" I asked. "I mean, *why* would he do something like that?"

"I think," Jesse said, "if we hurry, we might be able to find out."

He pointed. We looked. The clouds overhead had parted enough to allow us to see the tiny slice of beach at the bottom of the cliff. The moonlight picked out four ghostly forms huddled in a circle around a pitiful little campfire.

"Oh, God," I said as the clouds closed in again, quickly obscuring the sight. "All the way down there? I know I'm going to get bitten."

Father Dominic had already started hurrying down the rest of the trail. Jesse, behind me, asked curiously, "Bitten by what, Susannah?"

"A snake, of course," I said, avoiding a root that had looked a bit snakelike in the beam from my flashlight.

"Snakes," Jesse said—and I could tell by his voice that he was restraining an urge to laugh, "don't come out at night."

This was news to me. "They don't?"

"Not usually. And particularly not on cold, wet nights like this. They like the sun."

Well, that was a relief. Still, I couldn't help wondering about ticks. Did ticks come out at night?

It seemed to take forever—and I was sure that I'd wake up with shin splints—but we eventually reached the bottom of the path, though the last fifty feet or so were so steep, I practically sprinted down them, and not on purpose, either.

There on the beach, the sound of the waves was much, much louder—loud enough to completely drown out the sound of our approach. The smell of salt was heavy in the air. I realized, as our feet sank into the wet sand—well, except for Jesse's—why it was I hadn't seen any gulls earlier in the evening: animals, including birds, don't like ghosts.

And there were a lot of ghosts on this particular beach.

They were singing. I am not kidding you. They were singing around their sulky little fire. You won't believe what they were singing, either. "Ninety-nine Bottles of Beer on the Wall." Seriously. They were on fifty-seven.

I tell you, if that's how I end up spending eternity when I die, I hope some mediator comes along and puts me out of my misery. I really do.

"Okay," I said, slipping off my gloves and jamming them in my pockets. "Jesse, you take the guys. I'll take the girls. Father D, you just make sure none of them make a run for the waves, all right? I've already been swimming once today, and believe me, that water's cold. I am not going in after them."

Father Dominic caught my arm as I started striding toward the firelit group.

"Susannah!" he cried, looking genuinely shocked. "Surely you can't...you aren't seriously suggesting that we—"

"Father D." I gawked up at him. "Earlier this afternoon, those jerks over there tried to drown me. Pardon me if I feel that sauntering up to them and asking them if they'd like to join us for root beer floats isn't such a good idea. Let's go kick some supernatural butt."

Father Dominic only clutched my arm tighter. "Susannah, how many times do I have to tell you? We are mediators. Our job is to intercede on behalf of troubled souls, not cause them more pain and grief by committing acts of violence upon them—"

"I'll tell you what," I said. "Jesse and I will hold them down while you do the interceding. Because, believe me, that's the only way they're going to listen. They aren't real communicative."

"Susannah," Father Dom said again.

But this time, he didn't get to finish whatever it was he was going to say. That's because all of a sudden, Jesse went, "Stay here, both of you, until I say it's all right to move."

And then he started striding across the beach toward the ghosts.

Huh. I guess he'd gotten sick of listening to the two of us arguing. Well, you couldn't really blame him.

Father Dominic looked worriedly after Jesse. "Oh, dear," he said. "You don't think he's going to do anything...rash, do you, Susannah?"

I sighed. Jesse never did anything rash.

"No," I said. "He's probably just going to try to talk to them. It's better this way, I guess. I mean, he's a ghost, they're ghosts...they've got a lot of stuff in common."

"Ah," Father Dominic said, nodding. "Yes, I see. Very wise. Very wise indeed."

The Angels were at seventeen bottles of beer on the wall by the time they noticed Jesse.

One of the boys swore quite colorfully, but before any of them had time to dematerialize, Jesse was speaking—and in such a low voice that Father D and I couldn't hear him above the sound of the waves. We could only watch as Jesse—glowing a little, the way ghosts tend to—spoke to them, and then, slowly, after a little while, lowered himself into the sand, still talking.

Father Dominic, watching the proceedings intently, murmured, "Excellent idea, sending Jesse in first."

I shrugged. "I guess."

I guess my disappointment that I'd missed out on what probably would have been a first class brawl must have shown, since Father D tore his gaze from the group around the campfire, and grinned down at me.

"With a little help from Jesse, we just might make a mediator of you yet," he said.

As if he had a clue as to how many ghosts I'd mediated out of existence before I'd ever even met either of them, I thought. But I didn't say it out loud.

"And how," Father Dominic asked quietly, "is your little friend Gina occupying herself while you're out tonight?"

"Oh," I said. "She's covering for me."

Father Dominic raised his eyebrows—and his voice—in surprised disapproval. "Covering for you? Your parents don't know you're here?"

"Oh, yeah, Father D," I said sarcastically. "I told my mom I was coming out to Big Sur to deal with the ghosts of some dead teenagers. Please."

He looked troubled. Being a priest, Father D frowns on dishonesty, particularly when it involves parents, whom his ilk are always encouraging us to honor and obey. But I figure if God really wanted me heeding that particular rule, He wouldn't have made me a mediator. The two things just don't mix, you know?

"But evidently," Father Dominic said, "you had no trouble telling Gina."

"I didn't, actually. Tell her, I mean. She kind of just...knows. I mean, once she and I went to this psychic, and..." My voice trailed off. Talking about Madame Zara reminded me of what Gina had told me, about the whole one single love of a lifetime thing. Was it true? I wondered. Could it possibly be true? I shivered, but this time, it had nothing to do with the cold.

"I see," Father Dominic said. "Interesting. You

feel comfortable telling your friends about your extraordinary ability, but not your own mother."

We had had this argument before—recently, in fact—so I just rolled my eyes at him. "Friend," I corrected him. "Not *friends.* Gina knows. Nobody else. And she doesn't know *all* of it. She doesn't, for instance, know about Jesse."

Father Dominic glanced in the direction of the bonfire once again. Jesse appeared to be deeply engrossed in his conversation with Josh and the others. Their faces, orange in the firelight, were all turned in his direction, their gazes locked on him. It was strange they had built that fire. They couldn't feel it, any more than they could get drunk from the beer they'd tried to steal, or drown in the water they'd been under. I wondered why they had gone to the trouble. It had probably taken a lot of kinetic power to light it.

All four of them glowed with the same subtle light Jesse gave off—not enough to see by on a dark night like this, but enough to tell they weren't quite...well, *human* was the wrong word, because of course they were human. Or had been, anyway.

I guess the word I'm looking for is *alive.*

"Father D," I said, abruptly. "Do you believe in psychics? I mean, are they real? Like mediators?"

Father Dominic said, "I'm sure some of them are."

"Well," I went on in a rush before I could change my mind. "This psychic Gina and I went to once, she knew I was a mediator. I didn't tell her, or anything. She just knew. And she said this weird thing. At least, Gina says she did. I don't remember it. But according to Gina, she said I would only have one true love."

Father Dominic looked down at me. Was it my imagination, or did he look amused? "Were you planning on having a great many?"

"Well, not exactly," I said, a little embarrassed. You would have been, too. I mean, come on. The guy was a priest. "But it's kind of weird. This psychic—Madame Zara—she said a bunch of stuff about how I'd just have this one love, but that it would last for, like, my whole life." I swallowed. "Or maybe it was all eternity. I forget."

"Oh," Father Dominic said, not looking amused anymore. "Dear."

"That's what I said. I mean...well, she probably didn't know what she was talking about. Because that sounds kind of bogus, right?" I asked hopefully.

But much to my disappointment, Father D said, "No, Susannah. It does not sound bogus. Not to me."

He said it in such a way...I don't know. Something about the way he said it made me ask, curiously, "Were you ever in love, Father D?"

He started fumbling around in his coat pockets. "Um," he said.

I knew what he was looking for so intently: a pack of cigarettes. I also knew he wasn't going to find any—he had quit smoking years ago, and kept only one pack for emergencies. And that, I happened to know, was back in his office at the school.

I also knew, from the fact that he'd started looking for them at all, that Father D was stressed. He only felt an urge to smoke when things weren't quite going how he'd planned.

He had been in love. I could totally tell by the way he was avoiding meeting my gaze.

I wasn't really surprised. Father Dominic was old, and a priest, and everything, but he was still a hottie, in a senior citizen, Sean Connery kind of way.

"There was, I believe," he said finally, when his search came up negative, "a young woman. At one time."

Aha. I pictured Audrey Hepburn, for some reason. You know, in that movie that's always on, the one where she played a nun. Maybe Father Dom and his one true love had met in priest and nun school! Maybe their love had been forbidden like in the movie!

"Did you know her before you took your, um, orders, or whatever they're called?" I asked, trying to sound casual. "Or after?"

"Before, of course!" He sounded shocked. "For heaven's sake, Susannah."

"I was just wondering." I kept my gaze on Jesse over by the campfire, so Father D wouldn't be too embarrassed thinking I was staring at him, or anything. "I mean, we don't have to talk about it, if you don't want to." Only I couldn't help it. "Was she—"

"I was your age," Father Dominic said, as if he wanted to hurry up and get it over with. "In high school, like you. She was a little younger."

I had trouble picturing Father Dominic in high school. I didn't even know what color his hair had been before it turned the snowy white it was now.

"It was..." Father D went on, a faraway look in his bright blue eyes. "It...well, it would never have worked."

"I know," I said. Because suddenly I did know. I don't know how I knew, but something in the way he said it never would have worked just told me, I guess. "She was a ghost, right?"

Father Dominic inhaled so sharply that for a second I thought he was having a heart attack, or something.

But before I had a chance to jump in and start CPR, Jesse got up from the fire, and started coming toward us.

"Oh, look," Father Dominic said with obvious relief. "Here comes Jesse."

I had gotten over the annoyance I used to feel at Jesse when he'd appear suddenly, usually when I least expected—or wanted—him to. Now I was almost always glad to see him.

Except at that particular moment. At that particular moment, I wished Jesse was far, far away. Because I had a feeling I was never going to get Father D to open up about this particular subject again.

"All right," Jesse said, when he'd come close enough to speak to us. "I think they'll listen to you now, Father, without trying to bolt. They're quite frightened."

"They sure didn't act very frightened when they were trying to kill me this afternoon," I muttered.

Jesse looked down at me, a trace of amusement in his dark eyes—though what's so funny about me practically drowning, I don't know.

"I think," he said, "if you listen to what they have to say, you'll understand why they behaved the way they did."

"We'll see about that," I said with a sniff.

CHAPTER

12

I guess I was in kind of a bad mood because of Jesse interrupting my little heart-to-heart with Father Dominic. But that was no reason for him to come up behind me as I was walking toward the group around the fire and whisper, "Behave," in my ear.

I flashed him a look of annoyance. "I always do," I said.

You know what he did then? He laughed! And not in a very nice way, either. I couldn't believe it.

When I got close enough to the group to be able to make out the expressions on their faces, I didn't see anything to convince me they weren't still the same ghosts who'd tried to kill me—twice—in two days.

"Wait a minute," Josh said when he recognized me. He climbed quickly to his feet, and pointed accusingly at me. "That's the bitch who—"

Jesse stepped quickly into the firelit circle. "Now," he said, "I told you who these people were—"

"You said they were going to help us," Felicia

wailed from where she sat, the skirt of her evening dress poofing up all around her. "But that girl there kicked me in the face this afternoon!"

"Oh," I said, "like you weren't trying to drown me at the time?"

Father Dominic stepped quickly between me and the ghosts and said, "My children, my children, do not be alarmed. We are here to help you, if we can."

Josh Saunders, stunned, said, "You can see us?"

"I can," Father Dominic said solemnly. "Susannah and I are, as I'm sure Jesse explained, mediators. We can see you, and we want to help you. Indeed, it is our responsibility to help you. Only, you must understand, it is also our responsibility to ensure that you don't harm anyone. That is why Susannah tried to stop you earlier today, and, if I understand correctly, the day before."

This caused Mark Pulsford to say a bad word. Felicia Bruce elbowed him and said, "Cut it out. That guy's a priest."

Mark said, belligerently, "He is not."

"He is so," Felicia said. "Can't you see the little white thingie around his neck?"

"I *am* a priest." Father Dominic hastened to cut the argument short. "And I am telling you the truth. You can call me Father Dominic. And this is Susannah Simon. Now, we understand that the four of you feel a bit of resentment toward Mr. Meducci—"

"Resentment?" Josh, still standing, glared at Father Dominic. "*Resentment?* It's because of that jerk that we're all dead!"

Only he didn't say *jerk*.

Father Dominic raised his white eyebrows, but

Jesse said, calmly, "Why don't you tell the father what it was you told me, Josh, so that he and Susannah can begin to understand."

Josh, his bowtie hanging loosely around his neck, and the first few buttons of his dress shirt undone, lifted a hand and ran his fingers frustratedly through his short blond hair. He had obviously been, in life, an extremely good-looking boy. Blessed with looks, intelligence, and wealth (his parents had to have money if they could afford to send him to Robert Louis Stevenson School, which was as expensive as it was exclusive), Josh Saunders was having trouble adjusting to the only misfortune that had ever befallen him in his short, happy life:

His untimely death.

"Look," he said. The sounds of the waves, and now the crackle of the little fire they'd made, were easily drowned out by his deep voice. Had he lived, Josh might have been anything, I thought to myself, from professional athlete to president. He exuded that kind of confidence.

"On Saturday night we went to a dance," he said. "A *dance*, okay? And afterward, we thought we might go for a drive, and park—"

Carrie chimed in: "We always park at the Point on Saturday night."

"The observation point," Felicia explained.

"It's so pretty," Carrie said.

"Really pretty," Felicia said with a quick glance at Father Dominic.

I stared at them. Who were they kidding? We all knew what they were doing parked at the observation point.

And it wasn't looking at the view.

"Yeah," Mark said. "Plus no cops ever come by, and make us move. You know?"

Ah. Such honesty was refreshing.

"All right," Josh said. He had shoved his hands in his trouser pockets. Now he took them out, and held them, palms toward us. "So we went for this drive. Everything's going fine, right? Same as any other Saturday night. Only it wasn't the same. Because this last time, when we went around the corner—you know, that hairpin curve up there—something rammed us—"

"Yeah," Carrie said. "No lights, no warning, nothing. Just bam."

"We went right into the guardrail," Josh said. "No big deal. We weren't going very fast. I thought, Shit, I crushed the fender. And I started to back up. But then he hit us again—"

"Oh, but surely—" Father Dominic began.

Josh, however, went on as if the priest hadn't spoken.

"And the second time he hit us," Josh said, "we just kept on going."

"As if the guardrail weren't even there," Felicia put in.

"We went straight over." Josh slipped his hands back into his pockets. "And woke up down here. Dead."

There was silence after that. At least no one spoke. There was still the sound of the waves, of course, and the crackling of the fire. Spray from the sea, blown by the wind, was coating my hair and forming little ice crystals in it. I moved closer to the fire, thankful for its warmth...

And realized, all in a rush, why the RLS Angels had gone to the trouble of building it. Because that's what they'd have done if they'd still been alive. They'd have built a fire for warmth. So what if they could no longer feel its heat? It didn't matter. That's what live people would have done.

And all they wanted was to be alive again.

"Troubling," Father Dominic said. "Very troubling. But surely, my children, you can see that it was just an accident—"

"An accident?" Josh glared at Father D. "There was nothing *accidental* about it, Father. That guy—that Michael guy—came at us *on purpose.*"

"But that's ridiculous," Father Dominic said. "Perfectly ridiculous. Why on earth would he do such a thing?"

"Simple," Josh said with a shrug. "He's jealous."

"Jealous?" Father Dominic looked appalled. "Perhaps you aren't aware of this, young man, but Michael Meducci, whom I have known since he was in the first grade, is a very gifted student. He is well liked by his fellow classmates. Why in heaven's name would he— No. No, I'm sorry. You're mistaken, my boy."

I wasn't sure which universe Father Dom was living in—the one where Michael Meducci was well liked by his fellow classmates—but it sure wasn't this one. As far as I knew, no one at the Mission Academy liked Michael Meducci—or even knew him, outside of the chess club. But then, I had only been there a few months, so maybe I was wrong.

"He may be gifted," Josh said, "but he's still a geek."

Father Dominic blinked at him. "Geek?" he ventured.

"You heard me." Josh shook his head. "Look, Father, face facts. Your boy Meducci is nothing. *Nothing. We*"—he pointed at himself, then gestured toward his friends—"on the other hand, were *it*. The most popular people in our school. Nothing happened at RLS unless it had our seal of approval. A party wasn't a party until *we* got there. A dance wasn't a dance unless Josh, Carrie, Mark, and Felicia—the RLS 'Angels'—were there. Okay? Are you getting the picture now?"

Father Dominic looked confused. "Um," he said. "Not quite."

Josh rolled his eyes. "Is this guy for real?" he asked me and Jesse.

Jesse said, without smiling, "Very much so."

"Okay," Josh said. "Then let me put it to you this way. This Meducci guy? He may have the sparkling GPA. But so what? That's nothing. I've got a 4.0. I hold the school record in the high jump. I belong to the National Honor Society. I play forward on the basketball team. I've been president of the student council for three years in a row, and for a lark, this spring I tried out for—and got—the lead in the school drama society's production of *Romeo and Juliet*. Oh, and guess what? I was accepted to Harvard. Early decision."

Josh paused to take a breath. Father Dominic opened his mouth to say something, but Josh barreled right along.

"How many Saturday nights," Josh asked, "do you think Michael Meducci has sat alone in his room playing video games? Huh? Well, let me put it to you another way: do you know how many *I've* spent caressing a joystick? None. Want to know why? Because there's never been a Saturday night when I didn't have something to do—a party to go to or a girl to take out. And not just any girl, either, but the hottest, most popular girls in school. Carrie here"—he gestured at Carrie Whitman, sitting in the sand in her ice-blue evening gown—"models part-time up in San Francisco. She's done commercials. She was homecoming queen."

"Two years in a row," Carrie pointed out in her squeaky voice.

Josh nodded. "Two years in a row. Are you starting to get it now, Father? Is Michael Meducci dating a model? I don't think so. Is Michael Meducci's best friend like mine, Mark over there, captain of the football team? Does Michael Meducci have a full athletic scholarship to UCLA?"

Mark, obviously not the group genius, went, with feeling, "Go Bruins."

"What about me?" Felicia demanded.

Josh said, "Yes, what about Mark's girlfriend, Felicia? Head cheerleader, captain of the dance team, and, oh yeah, winner of a National Merit Scholarship because of her superior grades. So, keeping all that in mind, let's ask that question again, shall we? Why would a guy like Michael Meducci want people like us dead? Simple: he's jealous."

The silence that swept in after this statement was almost as penetrating as the smell of brine permeating the air. No one said a word. The Angels looked too self-righteous to speak, and Father Dom seemed stunned by their revelations. Jesse's feelings on the subject were unclear; he looked a little bored. I guess to a guy born over a hundred and fifty years ago, the words *National Merit Scholarship* don't mean much.

I pried my tongue from where it had been stuck to the roof of my mouth. I was very thirsty from my long hike down, and I certainly wasn't looking forward to the climb back up to Father Dom's car. But I felt compelled, despite my discomfort, to speak.

"Or," I said, "it could be because of his sister."

CHAPTER 13

Everyone—from Father Dom to Carrie Whitman—blinked at me in the firelight.

"Excuse me?" Josh said. Only his tone was more impatient than polite.

"Michael's sister," I said. "The one who's in the coma."

Don't ask me what made me think of it. Maybe it was Josh's reference to parties—how no party began until he and the other Angels got there. That started me thinking of the last party I'd heard about—the one where Michael's sister had fallen into the pool and nearly drowned. Some party that must have been. Had the police broken it up after the ambulance arrived?

Father Dominic's shaggy white eyebrows went up. "You mean Lila Meducci? Yes, of course. How could I have forgotten about her? It's tragic—very tragic—what happened to her."

Jesse piped up for the first time in some minutes. "What happened to her?" he asked, lifting his chin from the knee he'd been resting it on, his foot propped up against the boulder he was sitting on.

"An accident," Father Dom said, shaking his head. "A terrible accident. She tripped and fell into a swimming pool and very nearly drowned. Her parents are losing hope that she'll ever regain consciousness."

I grunted. "That's one version of the story, anyway," I said. Michael's parents had obviously cleaned it up for the principal of their daughter's school.

"You left out the part," I went on, "about how she was at a party in the Valley when it happened. And that she was completely blotto when she went under." I narrowed my eyes at the four ghosts seated on the opposite side of the fire. "So was everybody else at this particular party, apparently, since nobody noticed what happened to her until she'd been under long enough to curdle her brain." I looked at Jesse. "Did I mention the fact that she's only fourteen years old?"

Jesse, still sitting on the boulder, his hands around the propped up knee, looked at the Angels. "I don't suppose any of you," he said, "would know something about this."

Mark looked disgusted. "How would any of us know about some geek's sister getting wasted at a party?" he demanded.

"Perhaps because one—or all—of you happened to be at the party at the time?" I suggested sweetly.

Father Dominic looked startled. "Is this true?" He blinked down at the Angels. "Do any of you know anything about this?"

"Of course not," Josh said—too quickly, I

thought. Felicia's "As if" was not very convincing, either.

It was Carrie who gave it away, though.

"Even if we did," she demanded with unfeigned indignation, "what would it matter? Just because some stupid wannabe drank herself into a coma at one of our parties, how does that make *us* responsible?"

I stared at her. Felicia, I remembered, was the National Merit Scholar. Carrie Whitman had only been homecoming queen. Twice.

"How about, just for starters," I said, "making alcohol available to an eighth grader?"

"How were we supposed to know how old she was?" Felicia asked, not very nicely. "I mean, she had enough makeup slathered on, I could have sworn she was forty."

"Yeah," Carrie said. "And that particular party was by invitation only. I certainly never issued an invitation to any *eighth grader.*"

"If you want to hold someone responsible," Felicia said, "how about the idiot who brought her in the first place?"

"Yeah," Carrie said angrily.

"I don't think Susannah is the one holding you responsible for what happened to Michael's sister." Jesse's voice, after the shrillness of the girls, sounded like distant thunder. It shut the others up quite effectively. "Michael, I believe, is the one who killed you for it."

Father Dominic made a soft noise as if Jesse's words had sunk, like a fist, into his stomach.

"Oh, no," he said. "No, surely you can't think—"

"It makes more sense," Jesse said, "than this one's argument"—he nodded briefly at Josh—"that Michael did it out of jealousy because he has no... what is it? Oh, yes. Dates on Saturday night."

Josh looked uncomfortable. "Well," he said, tugging on his evening jacket's lapels. "I didn't know the skank they fished out of Carrie's pool was Meducci's sister."

"This," Father Dominic said, "is too much. Simply too much. I am...I am *appalled* by all of this."

I glanced at him, surprised by what I heard in his voice. It was—if I wasn't mistaken—pain. Father Dominic was actually hurt by what he'd just heard.

"A young girl is in a coma," he said, his blue-eyed gaze very bright as it bored into Josh, "and you call her names?"

Josh had the grace to look ashamed of himself. "Well," he said, "it's just a figure of speech."

"And you two." Father Dominic pointed at Felicia and Carrie. "You break the law by serving alcohol to minors, and dare to suggest that it is the girl's own fault she was harmed by it?"

Carrie and Felicia exchanged glances.

"But," Felicia said, "nobody else got hurt, and they were all drinking, too."

"Yeah," Carrie said. "Everybody was doing it."

"That doesn't matter." Father Dominic's voice was shaking with emotion now. "If everyone else jumped off the Golden Gate Bridge, would that make it right?"

Whoa, I thought. Father D obviously needed a little refresher course in student discipline if he thought that old line still had any punch.

And then my eyes widened as I noticed that Father Dominic was now pointing at me. *Me?* What had *I* done?

I soon found out.

"And you," Father Dominic said. "You still insist that what happened to these young people was not an accident, but deliberate murder!"

My jaw sagged. "Father D," I managed to say when I'd levered it back into place. "Excuse me, but it's pretty obvious—"

"It isn't." Father Dominic dropped his arm. "It isn't obvious to me. So the boy had motive? That doesn't make him a killer."

I glanced at Jesse for help, but it was apparent from his startled expression that he was as baffled by Father Dominic's outburst as I was.

"But the guardrail," I tried. "The loosened bolts—"

"Yes, yes," Father Dominic said, quite testily for him. "But you're missing the most important point, Susannah. Supposing Michael did lie in wait for them. Perhaps he did intend, when they turned that corner, to ram them. How was he able to tell, in the dark, that he had the right car? Tell me that, Susannah. Anyone could have come around that corner. How could Michael have known he had the right car? *How?*"

He had me there. And he knew it. I stood there, the wind from the sea whipping hair into my face, and looked at Jesse. He looked back at me, and gave a little shrug. He was at as much of a loss as I was. Father Dom was right. It didn't make any sense.

At least until Josh said, "The Macarena."

We all looked at him.

"I beg your pardon?" Father Dominic said. Even in anger, he was unerringly polite.

"Of course!" Felicia scrambled to her feet, tripping over her evening gown's long skirt. "Of course!"

Jesse and I exchanged yet another confused look. "The what?" I asked Josh.

"The Macarena," Josh said. He was smiling. Smiling, he didn't look anything like the guy who'd tried to drown me earlier that day. Smiling, he looked like what he was—a smart, athletic eighteen-year-old in the prime of his life.

Except that his life was over.

"I was driving my brother's car," he explained, still grinning. "He's away at college. He said I could use it while he was gone. It's bigger than my car. The only thing is, he had this stupid thing put in so that when you honk the horn it plays the Macarena."

"It's *so* embarrassing," Carrie informed us.

"And the night we were killed," Josh went on, "I laid on the horn as we were turning that corner—the one Michael was waiting behind."

"You're supposed to honk when you go around those hairpin curves," Felicia said, excitedly.

"And it played the Macarena." Josh's smile vanished as if wiped away by the wind. "And that's when he hit us."

"No other car horn on the peninsula," Felicia said, her expression no longer excited, "plays the Macarena. Not anymore. The Macarena was only hot for about the first two weeks after it came out. Then it became totally lame. Now they only play it at weddings and stuff."

"That's how he knew." Josh's voice was no longer filled with indignation. Now he merely sounded sad. His gaze was locked on the sea—a sea that was too dark to be distinguishable from the cloudy night sky. "That's how he knew it was us."

Frantically, I thought back to what Michael had told me, a few hours earlier, in his mother's minivan. *They came barreling around that corner.* That's what he'd said. *Didn't honk. Nothing.*

Only now Josh was saying they *had* honked. That not only had they honked, but that they had honked in a particular way, a way that distinguished Josh's car horn from all others....

"Oh," Father Dominic said, sounding as if he weren't feeling well. "Dear."

I totally agreed with him. Except...

"It still doesn't prove anything," I said.

"Are you kidding?" Josh looked at me as if *I* were the crazy one—like he wasn't wearing a tuxedo on the beach. "Of course it does."

"No, she's right." Jesse pushed himself off the boulder and came to stand beside Josh. "He has been very clever, Michael has. There is no way to prove—in a court of law, anyway—that he has committed a crime here."

Josh's jaw dropped. "What do you mean? He killed us! I'm standing here telling you so! We honked the horn, and he purposefully rammed us and pushed us over the cliff."

"Yes," Jesse said. "But your testimony will not hold up in a court of law, my friend."

Josh looked close to tears. "Why not?"

"Because it is the testimony," Jesse said evenly, "of a dead man."

Stung, Josh stabbed a finger in my direction. "*She*'s not dead. *She* can tell them."

"She can't," Jesse said. "What is she supposed to say? That she knows the truth about what happened that night because the ghosts of the victims told her? Do you think a jury will believe that?"

Josh glared at him. Then, his gaze falling to his feet, he muttered, "Well, fine then. We're right back to where we started. We'll just take the matter into our own hands, right, guys?"

"Oh, no, you don't," I said. "No way. Two wrongs do not make a right—and three most definitely don't."

Carrie glanced from me to Josh and back again. "What's she talking about?" she wanted to know.

"You are not," I said, "going to avenge your deaths by killing Michael Meducci. I am sorry. But that is just not going to happen."

Mark, for the first time all evening, rose to his feet. He looked at me, then at Jesse, and then at Father Dom. Then he went, "This is *bogus*, man," and started stalking off down the beach.

"So the geek's just going to get away with it?" Josh, his jaw set, glared menacingly at me. "He kills four people, and he gets off scot-free?"

"Nobody said that." Jesse, in the firelight, looked more grim-faced than I'd ever seen him. "But what happens to the boy isn't up to you."

"Oh, yeah?" Josh was back to sneering. "Who's it up to, then?"

Jesse nodded at Father Dominic and me. "Them," he said quietly.

"Them?" Felicia's voice rose on a disgusted note. "Why *them?"*

"Because they are the mediators," Jesse said. In the orange glow from the fire, his eyes looked black. "It's what they do."

CHAPTER 14

The only problem was that the mediators couldn't figure out just how, exactly, to handle the situation.

"Look," I whispered as Father Dominic dropped a white candle into the box I was holding, and dug out a purple one. "Let me just call the police with an anonymous tip. I'll tell them I was driving along Big Sur that night, and that I saw the whole thing, and that it was no accident."

Father Dominic screwed the purple candle into the place where the white one had been.

"And do you think the police follow up on every anonymous tip they receive?" He didn't bother whispering because there was no one to overhear us. The only reason I'd lowered my voice was because the basilica, with all its gold leaf and majestic stained glass, made me really nervous.

"Well, at least maybe they'll get suspicious." I followed Father Dominic as he climbed down from the stepladder, folded it up, and moved to the next Station of the Cross. "I mean, maybe they'll start looking into it a little more, bring Michael in for questioning, or something. I swear he'd crack if they'd just ask the right questions."

Father Dominic lifted the skirt of his black robe as he climbed back onto the ladder.

"And what," he asked, swapping another white candle for one of the purple ones in the box I was holding, "would the right questions be?"

"I don't know." My arms were getting tired. The box I was carrying was really heavy. Normally the novices would have been the ones changing the candles. Father Dominic, however, had been unable to keep still since our little field trip the night before, and had volunteered his services to the monsignor. *Our* services, I should say, since he'd dragged me out of religion class to help. Not that I minded. Being a devout agnostic, I wasn't getting all that much out of religion class, anyway—something Sister Ernestine hoped to rectify before I graduated.

"I think that the police," Father Dom said as he gave the candle a determined twist since it didn't seem to be fitting too easily into the holder, "can get along fine without our help. If what your mother said was true, the police seem suspicious enough of Michael already that it shouldn't be much longer before they bring him in for questioning."

"But what if my mom's just overreacting?" I noticed a tourist nearby, in madras and an Izod, admiring the stained glass windows, and lowered my voice even more. "I mean, she's a mom. She does that. Supposing the police don't really suspect anything at all?"

"Susannah." The candle successfully in place, Father Dominic climbed back down the ladder, and looked at me with an expression that appeared to be a mingling of exasperation and affection. There were, I noticed, purple shadows under Father Dom's eyes. We had both been pretty wiped after our long hike down to the beach and then back up again—not to mention the emotional wear and tear we'd experienced while we'd been down there.

Still, Father Dominic seemed to have sprung back with more vigor than you might expect for a guy in his sixties. *I* could barely walk, my shins ached so badly, and I couldn't stop yawning since our little tête-à-tête with the Angels had lasted until well past midnight. Father Dom, except for the shadows beneath his eyes, seemed almost sprightly, bubbling over with energy.

"Susannah," he said again, less exasperatedly, and more affectionately this time. "Promise me you will do nothing of the kind. You will not call the police with any anonymous tips."

I shifted the box of candles in my arms. It had certainly seemed like a good idea when I'd come up with it around four that morning. I'd lain awake almost all night wondering what on earth we were going to do about the RLS Angels and Michael Meducci.

"But—"

"And you will not, under any circumstances"—Father Dominic, apparently noticing my problem with the box, lifted it easily from my arms and set it down on the stepladder's top rung—"attempt to speak with Michael yourself about any of this."

That, of course, had been Plan B. If the whole anonymous tip thing to the cops didn't pan out, I'd planned on cornering Michael and sweet-talking—or beating, whichever proved most effective—a confession out of him.

"You will let me handle this," Father Dominic said loudly enough so that the tourist in the madras, who'd been about to take a picture of the altar, hastily lowered his camera and moved away. "I intend to speak to the young man, and I can assure you that if he is indeed guilty of this heinous crime—" I sucked in my breath, but Father Dominic held up a warning finger.

"You heard me," he said, a bit more quietly, but only because he'd noticed that one of the novices had slipped into the church carrying more black material to drape over the basilica's many statues of the Virgin Mary. They would remain cloaked in that manner, I had gathered, until Easter. Religion. That is some wacky stuff, let me tell you.

"If Michael is guilty of what those young people say he is, then I will convince him to confess." Father Dominic looked like he meant it, too. In fact, I hadn't even done anything, but somehow, looking at his stern expression, I wanted to confess. Once I had taken five dollars from my mother's wallet to buy a jumbo bag of Skittles. Maybe I could confess that.

"Now," Father Dominic said, pulling back the sleeve of his black robe and looking at his Timex. They don't pay priests enough for them to be able to get cool watches. "I am expecting Mr. Meducci to join me here momentarily, so you need to move along. It would be best for him not to see us together, I think."

"Why not? He has no idea we spent most of last night in conversation with his victims."

Father Dominic put a hand in the center of my

back and pushed. "Run along now, Susannah," he said in a fatherly sort of voice.

I went, but not very far. As soon as Father D's back was turned, I ducked down into a pew and crouched there, waiting. Waiting for what, I couldn't say. Well, all right, I could say: I was waiting for Michael. I wanted to see if Father D really would be able to get him to confess.

I didn't have to wait long. About five minutes later, I heard Michael's voice say, not too far from where I was hiding, "Father Dominic? Sister Ernestine said you wanted to speak to me."

"Ah, Michael." Father Dominic's voice conveyed none of the horror that I knew he felt over the prospect of one of his students being a possible murderer. He sounded relaxed and even jovial.

I heard the box of candles rattle.

"Here," Father Dominic said. "Hold those, will you?"

He had, I realized, just handed Michael the box I'd been holding.

"Uh," Michael said. "Sure, Father Dominic."

I heard the scrape of the stepladder being folded again. Father Dom was picking it up and moving to the next Station of the Cross. I could still hear him, however...barely.

"I've been worried about you, Michael," Father Dominic said. "I understand that your sister isn't showing much sign of improvement."

"No, Father," Michael said. His voice was so soft, I could hardly hear it.

"I'm very sorry to hear that. Lila is a very sweet girl. I know you must love her very much."

"Yes, Father," Michael said.

"You know, Michael," Father Dominic said. "When bad things happen to the people we love, we often...well, sometimes we turn our backs on God."

Aw, geez, I thought, from my pew. That wasn't the way. Not with *Michael.*

"Sometimes we become so resentful that this terrible thing has happened to someone who doesn't deserve it that we not only turn our backs on God, but we might even begin contemplating...well, things we wouldn't ordinarily contemplate if the tragedy hadn't occurred. Like, for instance, revenge."

All right, I thought. Getting better, Father D.

"Miss Simon."

Startled, I looked around. The novice who had come in to finish draping the statues was staring at me from the end of my pew.

"Oh," I said. I slithered up off of my knees and into the seat. Father Dominic and Michael, I saw, had moved so that their backs were to me. They were too far away to overhear us.

"Hi," I said to the novice. "I was just, um, looking for an earring."

The novice didn't appear to believe me.

"Don't you have religion with Sister Ernestine right now?" she asked.

"Yes, Sister," I said. "I do."

"Well, hadn't you better get to class, then?"

Slowly, I rose to my feet. It wouldn't have mattered, even if I hadn't gotten caught. Father Dominic and Michael had moved too far away for me to have heard anything anyway.

I walked, with what dignity I could, toward the end of the pew, pausing when I reached the novice before moving on.

"Sorry, Sister," I said. Then, striving to break the awkward silence that ensued, during which the novice stared at me in mute disapproval, I added, "I like your, um..."

But since I couldn't remember what they call that dress they all wear, the compliment fell a little flat, even though I thought I'd sort of saved it at the end by gesturing toward her and going, "You know, your thing. It's very figure flattering."

But I guess that's the wrong thing to say to somebody who is in training to be a nun, since the novice got very red in the face and said, "Don't make me have to report you again, Miss Simon."

Which I thought was sort of harsh, considering I'd been trying, anyway, to be nice. But whatever. I left the church and headed back to class, taking the long way, through the brightly sunlit courtyard, so I could soothe my frazzled nerves by listening to the sound of the burbling fountain.

My nerves soon shot back up to frazzled, however, when I spotted another one of the novices standing by the statue of Father Serra, delivering a little lecture to a group of tourists about the missionary's good works. In order to avoid being spotted out of class without a hall pass (why hadn't I thought to ask Father D for one? I'd been thrown by the whole candle thing), I ducked into the girls' room, where I was met by a cloud of gray smoke.

Which meant only one thing, of course.

"Gina," I said, stooping over so I could figure out

which stall she was in by looking under the doors. "Are you insane?"

Gina's voice came floating out from one of the stalls on the end, near the window, which she'd strategically opened.

"I do not," she said, throwing open the stall door, and then hanging onto it while she puffed, "believe so."

"I thought you quit smoking."

"I did." Gina joined me on the window sill, onto which I'd hauled myself. The Mission, having been built in like the year 1600 or something, was made of this really thick adobe, so all the windows were set back two feet into the stone. This supplied built-in window seats that, if they were a little high, were at least very cool and comfortable.

"I only smoke now in emergencies," Gina explained. "Like during religion class. You know I am philosophically opposed to organized religion. How about you?"

I raised my eyebrows. "I don't know," I said. "Buddhism has always struck me as kind of cool. That whole reincarnation thing is very appealing."

"That's Hinduism, you dink," Gina said. "And I was talking about smoking."

"Oh. Okay. No, I never got the hang of it. Why?" I grinned at her. "Didn't Sleepy tell you about the time he caught me trying to smoke?"

She frowned prettily. "He did not. And I wish you wouldn't call him that."

I made a face. "Jake, then. He was pretty peeved about it. You better not let him catch you at it, or he'll dump you like a hot potato."

"I highly doubt that," Gina said with a mysterious smile.

She was probably right. I wondered what it would be like to be Gina, and have every boy you met fall madly in love with you. The only boys who fell madly in love with me were boys like Michael Meducci. And he wasn't even technically in love with me. He was in love with the idea that I was in love with him. Something I still couldn't think about, by the way, without shuddering.

I heaved a dejected sigh and looked out the window. About a mile of sloping, cypress-tree-dotted landscape stretched to the sea, teal blue and sparkling in the bright afternoon sunlight.

"I don't see how you can stand it." Gina exhaled a plume of gray smoke. She was back to talking about religion class, I could tell from her tone. "I mean, it must all *really* seem bogus to you, considering the whole mediator thing."

I shrugged. I had gotten home too late the night before for Gina and I to have our "talk." She'd been sound asleep when I snuck back into the house. Which was just as well, since I'd been exhausted.

Not exhausted enough, however, to fall asleep.

"I don't know," I said. "I mean, I haven't got the slightest idea where the ghosts go after I send them packing. They just...go. Maybe to heaven. Maybe on to their next life. I doubt I'll ever know until I die myself."

Gina aimed her next plume of smoke out the window. "You make it," she said, "sound like a trip. Like when we die, we're just moving to a new address."

"Well," I said. "Personally, I think that's how it

works. Just don't ask me to tell you what that address is. Because that I don't know."

"So." Her cigarette finished, Gina stamped it out on the adobe beneath us, then flung the butt expertly over the closest stall door, and into the toilet. I heard the plop, and then the sizzle. "What was that all about last night, anyway?"

I told her. About the RLS Angels, and how they thought Michael had killed them. I told her about Michael's sister, and the accident out on the Pacific Coast Highway. I told her about how Josh and his friends were looking to avenge their deaths, and about how Father Dominic and I had argued with them, long into the night, until we'd finally convinced them to let us try to bring Michael to justice the old-fashioned way—you know, utilizing the appropriate law enforcement agencies, and not a paranormal contract killing.

There was only one thing I didn't tell her, and that was about Jesse. For some reason, I just couldn't bring myself to mention him. Maybe because of what the psychic had said. Maybe because I was afraid Madame Zara was right, that I really was this giant loser who was only going to fall in love with one person my entire life, and that person was a guy who:

(a) did not love me back, and

(b) wasn't exactly someone I could introduce to my mother, since he wasn't even alive.

Or maybe it was simply because...well, maybe because Jesse was a secret I wanted to hug to myself, like some stupid girl with a crush on Carson Daly, or somebody. Maybe someday I'd take to standing underneath my bedroom window with a big sign that says *Jesse, will you go to prom with me?* like all those girls who stand around outside the MTV studios, though I sincerely hoped someone would shoot me or something before it comes to that.

When I was through, Gina sighed, and said, "Well, it just goes to show. The cute ones always do end up being psychotic murderers."

She meant Michael.

"Yeah," I said. "But he's not even that cute. Except with his clothes off."

"You know what I mean." Gina shook her head. "What are you going to do if he doesn't confess to Father Dominic?"

"I don't know." This was something that had contributed to my insomnia of the night before. "I guess we'll just have to get some proof."

"Oh, yeah? Where you gonna find that? The evidence store?" Gina yawned, looked at her watch, and then hopped off the window sill. "Two minutes until lunch," she said. "What do you think it will be today? Corn dogs again?"

"It always is," I said. The Mission Academy was not exactly known for the culinary excellence of its cafeteria. That was because it didn't have one. We ate lunch outside, out of these vendor wagons. It was bizarre, even to a couple of chicks from Brooklyn who had seen it all...as was illustrated by Gina's total lack of surprise about everything that I'd just told her.

"What I want to know," she said as we made our way out of the girls' room and into the soon-to-be-flooded-with-humanity breezeway, "is why you never said anything about any of this stuff before.

You know, the mediator stuff. It wasn't as if I didn't know."

You *don't* know, I thought. Not the worst part, anyway.

"I was afraid you'd tell your mother," was what I said out loud. "And that she'd tell my mother. And that my mother would stick me in the loony bin. For my own good, of course."

"Of course," Gina said. She blinked down at me. "You are an idiot. You know that, don't you? I never would have told my mother. I never tell my mother anything, if I can avoid it. And I certainly wouldn't ever have told her—or anybody else, for that matter—about the mediator thing."

I shrugged uncomfortably. "I know," I said. "I guess...well, back then I was pretty uptight about everything. I guess I've loosened up some since then."

"They say California does that to people," Gina observed.

And then the Mission clock struck twelve. All of the classroom doors around us were flung open, and a flood of people started streaming toward us.

It only took about thirty seconds for Michael to find and then glom on to me.

"Hey," he said, not looking at all like somebody who had just confessed to a quadruple murder. "I've been looking for you. What are you doing after school today?"

"Nothing," I said quickly, before Gina could open her mouth.

"Well, the insurance company finally came through with a rental for me," Michael said, "and I was thinking, you know, if you wanted to go back to the beach, or something...."

Back to the beach? Did this guy have amnesia, or what? You'd think after what had happened to him the last time he'd gone to the beach, it'd be the one place he *wouldn't* want to go.

Still, though he didn't know it, he'd be perfectly safe there. This was on account of Jesse. He was keeping an eye on the Angels while Father Dom and I tried our hand at bringing their alleged killer to justice.

It was as I was mulling over a reply to this offer that I caught a glimpse of Father Dominic as he came toward us down the breezeway. Right before he was pulled into the teachers' lounge by an enthusiastically gesticulating Mr. Walden, he shook his head. Michael was standing with his back to him, so he didn't see. But Father Dom's message to me was clear:

Michael hadn't confessed.

Which meant only one thing: it was time to bring in the professionals.

Me.

"Sure," I said, looking from Father Dom back to Michael. "Maybe you can help me with my geometry homework. I don't think I'm ever going to get the hang of this stupid Pythagorean theorem. I swear I'm going to flunk out after that last quiz."

"The Pythagorean theorem isn't hard," Michael said, looking amused by my frustration. "The sum of the squares of the lengths of the sides of a right triangle is equal to the square of the length of the hypotenuse."

I went, "Huh?" in this helpless way.

"Look," Michael said. "I aced geometry. Why don't you let me tutor you?"

I looked up at him in what I hoped he would mistake for worshipfulness. "Oh, would you?"

"Sure," he said.

"Can we start today?" I asked. "After school?" I should get an Oscar. I really should. I had the whole helpless female thing totally down. "At your house?"

Michael only looked a little taken aback. "Um," he said. "Sure." Then, when he'd recovered from his surprise, he added, slyly, "My parents won't be home, though. My dad'll be at work, and my mom spends most of her time at the hospital. With my sister. You know. I hope that won't be a problem."

I did everything but flutter my eyelashes at him. "Oh, no," I said. "That'll be fine."

He looked pleased—and yet at the same time a little uncomfortable.

"Um," he said, as the hordes of people pushed past us. "Look, about lunch. I can't sit with you today. I've got some stuff to do. But I'll meet you here right after last period. Okay?"

I went, "Okay," in this total imitation of Kelly Prescott at her most school-spirited. It must have worked, since Michael went away looking dazed, but pleased.

That was when Gina grabbed my arm, pulled me into a doorway, and hissed, "What are you, high? You're going to the guy's *house? Alone?*"

I tried to shake her off. "Calm down, G," I said. Sleepy's nickname for her was kind of catchy, loath as I was to admit anything my stepbrother had come up with might have any sort of merit. "This is what I do."

"Hang out with possible murderers?" Gina looked skeptical. "I don't think so, Suze. Did you clear this with Father Dominic?"

"G," I said. "I'm a big girl. I can take care of myself."

She narrowed her eyes. "You didn't, did you? What are you, freelancing? And don't call me G."

"Look," I said, in what I hoped was a soothing tone. "Chances are, Michael won't say a word about it to me. But he's a geek, right? A computer geek. And what do computer geeks do when they're planning something?"

Gina still looked angry. "I don't know," she said. "And I don't care. I'm telling—"

"They write stuff down," I said calmly. "On their computer. Right? They keep a journal, or they brag to people in chat rooms, or they pull up schematics of the building they want to blow up, or whatever. So even if I can't get him to admit anything, if I can get some time alone with Michael's computer, I bet I can—"

"G!" Sleepy strolled up to us. "There you are. You doing lunch now?"

Gina's lips were pressed together in annoyance with me, but Sleepy did not appear to notice this. Neither did Dopey, who showed up a second later.

"Hey," he said breathlessly. "What are you guys just standing here for? Let's go eat."

Then he noticed me and sneered. "Suze, where's your shadow?"

I said with a sniff, "Michael will be unable to join

us for lunch today, having been unavoidably detained."

"Yeah," Dopey said, and then he made a rude remark pertaining to Michael's having been detained by an inability to get certain parts of his body back into his pants. This was apparently an allusion to Michael's lack of coordination and not an intimation that he was more endowed than the average sixteen-year-old male.

I chose to ignore this remark, as did Gina, though I think this was because she hadn't even heard it.

"I sure hope you know what you're doing," was all she said, and it was clear she was not speaking to either of my stepbrothers, which puzzled them enormously. Why would any girl bother speaking to *me* when she could be speaking to *them?*

"G," I said with some surprise. "What do you take me for? An amateur?"

"No," Gina said. "A fool."

I laughed. I really did think she was just being funny. It wasn't until much later that I realized there wasn't anything amusing about it at all.

Because it turned out Gina was one hundred percent right.

CHAPTER

15

Here's the thing about killers. If you know one, I'm sure you'll agree with me:

They can't help bragging about what they've done.

Seriously. They are totally vain. And that, generally, is their undoing.

Look at it from their point of view: I mean, here they are, and they've gotten away with this terrific crime. You know, something totally ingenious that no one would ever think to pin on them.

And they can't tell anybody. They can't tell a soul.

That's what gets them almost every time. Not telling anyone—not letting anyone in on their brilliant secret—well, that just about kills them.

Don't get me wrong. They don't want to get caught. They just want somebody to appreciate the brilliance of this thing they've done. Yes, it was a heinous—sometimes even unthinkable—crime. But look. *Look.* They did it *without getting caught.* They fooled the police. They fooled everybody. They *have* to tell somebody. They have to. Otherwise, what's the point?

This is just a personal observation, of course. I have met quite a few killers in my line of work, and this is the one thing they all seem to have in common. Only the ones who kept their mouths shut were the ones who managed to keep from getting caught. Everybody else? Slammer city.

So it seemed to me that Michael—who already believed that I was in love with him—just might decide to brag to me about what he'd done. He'd already started to, a little, when he'd told me how Josh and people like him were just a "waste of space." It seemed likely that, with a little prompting, I could get him to elaborate...maybe to the tune of a confession that I could then turn around and give to the police.

What's that you're saying? Guilty? Won't I feel guilty for snitching on this guy who had, after all, only been trying to get back at the kids who'd let his sister hurt herself so badly?

Yeah. Right. Listen, I don't do guilt. In my book, there are two kinds of people. Good ones and bad ones. As far as I was concerned, in this particular case, there wasn't a single good person to be found. Everybody had done something reprehensible, from Lila Meducci crashing that party and getting herself trashed in the process, to the RLS Angels for throwing the drunken free-for-all in the first place. Maybe some of them had committed crimes a little more heinous than the others—Michael's killing four people comes to mind—but frankly, in my mind...they all sucked.

So, in answer to your question, no, I didn't feel guilty about what I was about to do. The way I saw it, the sooner Michael got what was coming to him, the sooner I could get back to what was really important in life: lying on the beach with my best friend, soaking up some rays.

It was as I was in the girls' room just after last period let out, applying eyeliner in the mirror above the sinks—I have found that wringing confessions from potential murderers is easier when I am looking my best—that I got my first indication that the afternoon was not going to go exactly as I'd planned.

The door opened and Kelly Prescott walked in, followed by her shadow, Debbie Mancuso. They were not, apparently, there either to relieve or coif themselves, since all they did was stand there and stare at me in a hostile manner.

I looked at their reflections in the mirror and went, "If this is about funding for a class trip to the wine country, you can forget it. I already spoke to Mr. Walden about it, and he said it was the most ludicrous thing he'd ever heard of. Six Flags Great Adventure, maybe, but not the Napa Valley. Wineries *do* card, you know."

Kelly's upper lip curled. "This isn't about *that,*" she said in a disgusted tone of voice.

"Yeah," Debbie said. "This is about your *friend.*"

"My friend?" I had extracted a hairbrush from my backpack, and now I ran it through my hair, feigning unconcern. And I wasn't concerned. Not really. I could handle anything Kelly Prescott and Debbie Mancuso dished out. Only I didn't exactly feel like dealing with this, on top of everything else that had happened lately. "You mean Michael Meducci?"

Kelly rolled her eyes. "As if. Why you would ever want to be seen with *that,* I cannot imagine. But we happen to be talking about this Gina person."

"Yeah," Debbie said, her eyes narrowed to angry little slits.

Gina? Oh, *Gina.* Gina, who had stolen both Kelly's and Debbie's inamoratos. Suddenly all became clear.

"When is she going back to New York?" Kelly demanded.

"Yeah," Debbie said. "And where is she sleeping? Your room, right?"

Kelly elbowed her, and Debbie went, "Well, don't act like you don't want to know, Kel."

Kelly shot her friend an annoyed look, and then asked me, "There hasn't been any...well, bed-hopping, has there?"

Bed-hopping?

"Not to my knowledge," I said. I thought about messing with them, but the thing was, I really did feel for them. I know if some superhot femme fatale ghost had come along and stolen Jesse from me, I'd have been plenty peeved. Not that Jesse had ever even been mine to begin with.

"No bed-hopping," I said. "Footsie under the dinner table, maybe, but no bed-hopping that I know of."

Debbie and Kelly exchanged glances. I could see they were relieved.

"And she's leaving when?" Kelly asked.

When I said "Sunday," both girls let out a little sigh. Debbie went, "Good."

Now that she knew she wouldn't have to put up with her much longer, Kelly was willing to be gracious about Gina. "It isn't that we don't like her," she said.

"Yeah," Debbie said. "It's just that she's...you know."

"I know," I said in what I hoped was a comforting manner.

"It's just because she's new," Kelly said. Now she was getting defensive. "That's the only reason they like her. Because she's different."

"Sure," I said, putting my hairbrush back.

"I mean, so she's from New York?" Kelly was really warming to her subject. "Big deal. I mean, I've been to New York. It wasn't so great. It was really dirty, and there were these disgusting pigeons and bums everywhere."

"Yeah," Debbie said. "And you know what I heard? In New York, they don't even have fish tacos."

I almost felt sorry for Debbie then.

"Well," I said, shouldering my backpack. "It's been a pleasure. But now I gotta go, ladies."

I left them there, dipping their pinkies into little pots of lip gloss and then leaning into the mirror to apply it.

Michael was waiting for me exactly where he'd said he would be. You could tell the eyeliner was doing its job, since he got very flustered and went, "Hi, uh, do you, uh, want me to take your backpack?"

I cooed, "Oh, that would be lovely," and let him

take it. With two backpacks slung over his shoulders, mine and his own, Michael looked a bit odd, but then, he always did—at least with his clothes on—so this was no big surprise. We started down the cool, shady breezeway—empty now that most everybody had left for the day—and then stepped out into the warm yellow sunlight of the parking lot. The sea, just beyond it, winked at us. The sky overhead was cloudless.

"My car's over there," Michael said, pointing at an emerald green sedan. "Well, not my car, really. But the one the rental agency loaned me. It's not a bad little number, actually. Has some punch to it."

I smiled at him, and he tripped over a loose piece of concrete. He would have fallen flat on his face if he hadn't saved himself at the last minute. My lipstick, I could see, was performing as well as the eyeliner.

"Let me just, uh, find the keys," Michael said as he fumbled around in his pockets.

I told him to take his time. Then I pulled out my DKs and turned my face toward the sun, leaning against the hood of his rental car. How, I wondered, to best bring it up? Maybe I should suggest we stop by the hospital to see his little sister? No, I wanted to get to his house as soon as possible so I could start reading his email. Would I even know how to access his email? Probably not. But I could call Cee Cee. She'd know. Could you talk on the phone and access someone's email at the same time? Oh, God, why wouldn't my mom let me get a cell phone? I was practically the only sophomore without one—Dopey excepted, of course.

It was while I was wondering about this that a

shadow fell over my face, and suddenly I could no longer feel the warmth of the sun. I opened my eyes, and found myself staring up at Sleepy.

"What," he demanded in the same somnambulistic manner in which he did everything, "do you think you're doing?"

I could feel my cheeks getting red. And it wasn't because of the sun, either.

"Getting a ride home with Michael," I said meekly. I could see out of the corner of my eye that Michael, over on the driver's side of the car, had finally found the keys, and had frozen with them in his hand, the driver side door open.

"No, you're not," Sleepy said.

I couldn't believe it. I couldn't believe he was doing this to me. I was so embarrassed, I thought I was going to die.

"Slee—" I started to say, then stopped myself just in time. *"Jake,"* I said, under my breath. "Cut it *out.*"

"No," Jake said. *"You* cut it out. You remember what Mom said."

Mom. He'd called my mother *Mom.* What was going on here?

I lowered my sunglasses and looked past Jake. Gina, along with Dopey and Doc, stood on the far side of the parking lot, leaning against the side of the Rambler and staring in my direction.

Gina. She'd told on me. She'd told on me to *Sleepy.* I couldn't believe it.

"Slee—I mean, Jake," I said. "I appreciate your concern. I really do. But I can take care of myself—"

"No." And to my surprise, he wrapped a hand around my arm, and started to pull. He was surprisingly strong, for someone who gave the impression of being so tired all the time. "You're coming home with us. Sorry, man." This last he said to Michael. "She's supposed to ride home with me today."

Michael, however, did not appear to find this apology a satisfactory one. He put down both our backpacks, and, slipping his car keys back into his trouser pocket, took a step toward Sleepy.

"I don't think," Michael said in a hard voice I'd never heard him use before, "the lady wants to go with you."

The lady? What lady? Then I realized with a start that Michael meant me. *I* was the lady!

"I don't care what she wants," Sleepy said. His voice wasn't hard at all. It was simply very matter-of-fact. "She's not getting into a car with you, and that's the end of it."

"I don't think so." Michael took another step toward Sleepy, and that's when I saw that both of his hands were curled into fists.

Fists! Michael was going to fight Sleepy! Over me!

This was very exciting. I'd never had two boys get into a fight over me before. The fact that one of the boys was my stepbrother, however, and held about as much romantic appeal for me as Max, the family dog, somewhat dampened my enthusiasm.

And Michael wasn't much of a catch, either, when you actually thought about it, being a potential murderer, and all.

Oh, why did I have to have such a couple of losers fighting over me? Why couldn't Matt Damon and Ben Affleck fight over me? Now *that* would be truly excellent.

"Look, buddy," Sleepy said, noticing Michael's fists. "You don't want to mess with me, okay? I'm just going to take my sister here"—he dragged me off the hood of the car—"and go. Got that?"

Sister? *Step*sister! *Step*sister! God, why can't anyone keep it straight?

"Suze," Michael said. He hadn't taken his eyes off Sleepy. "Just get in the car, okay?"

Well, this, I decided, had gone on long enough. Not only was I completely embarrassed, but I was getting hot, too. That afternoon sun was no joke. Suddenly, I just didn't have any ghost-busting energy left in me.

Plus I guess I didn't want to see anybody get hurt over something so completely lame.

"Look," I said to Michael. "I better go with him. Some other time, okay?"

Michael finally looked away from Sleepy. His gaze, when it landed on me, was odd. It was like he wasn't even really seeing me.

"Fine," he said.

Then he got into his car without another word, and started the engine.

God, I thought. Be a baby about it, why don't you?

"I'll call you when I get home," I shouted to Michael, though I doubt he heard me through the rolled up windows. It would be difficult, I realized, to wring a confession out of him over the phone, but not, I thought, impossible.

Michael's tires squealed on the hot asphalt as he drove away.

"What a freakin' jerk," Sleepy muttered as he dragged me across the parking lot. Only he didn't say *freakin'*. Or *jerk*. "And you want to go out with this guy?"

I said sullenly, "We're just friends."

"Yeah," Sleepy said. "Right."

"You," Dopey said to me as Sleepy and I approached the Rambler, "are so busted."

This was one of his favorite things to say to me. He said it, as a matter of fact, whenever he had the slightest chance.

"Not technically, Brad," Doc said thoughtfully. "You see, she didn't actually get into the car with him. And that was what she was forbidden to do. Get into a car with Michael Meducci."

"Shut up, all of you," Sleepy said, heading for the driver's seat. "And get in."

Gina, I noticed, slipped automatically into the front passenger seat. Apparently, she didn't believe that when Sleepy had told us all to shut up, he meant her, too, since she went, "How about we stop somewhere for ice cream on the way home?"

She was trying, I knew, to get me not to be mad at her. As if a chocolate-dipped twist would help. Actually, it sort of would, now that I thought about it.

"Sounds good to me," Sleepy said.

Dopey, on my right—as usual, I'd ended up sitting on the hump in the middle of the backseat—muttered, "I don't know what you see in that headcase Meducci anyway."

Doc said, "Oh, that's easy. Females of any species tend to select the male partner who is best able to provide for her and any offspring which might result from their coupling. Michael Meducci, being a good deal more intelligent than most of his classmates, amply fulfills that role, in addition to which he has what is considered, by Western standards of beauty, an outstanding physique—if what I've overheard Gina and Suze saying counts for anything. Since he is likely to pass on these favorable genetic components to his children, he is irresistible to breeding females everywhere—at least, discerning ones like Suze."

There was silence in the car...the kind of silence that usually followed one of Doc's speeches.

Then Gina said reverently, "They really should move you up a grade, David."

"Oh, they've offered," Doc replied, cheerfully, "but while my intellect might be evolved for a boy my age, my growth is somewhat retarded. I felt it was inadvisable to thrust myself into a population of males much larger than I, who might be threatened by my superior intelligence."

"In other words," Sleepy translated for Gina's benefit, "we didn't want him getting his butt kicked by the bigger kids."

Then he started the car, and we roared out of the parking lot at the usual high rate of speed that Sleepy, in spite of my private nickname for him, chooses to employ.

I was trying to figure out how I could make it clear that it wasn't so much that I wanted to breed with Michael Meducci, as get him to confess to having killed the RLS Angels, when Gina went, "God, Jake, drive much?"

Which was sort of amusing since Gina, whose parents very wisely won't let her near their car, has never driven before in her life. But then I looked up and saw what she meant. We were approaching the front gates to the school, which were set at the base of a sloping hill that opened out into a busy intersection, at a higher rate of speed than was usual, even for Sleepy.

"Yeah, Jake," Dopey said from beside me on the backseat. "Slow down, you maniac."

I knew Dopey was only trying to make himself look good in front of Gina, but he did have a point: Sleepy was going way too fast.

"It's not a race," I said, and Doc started to say something about how Jake's endorphins had probably kicked in, due to his fight with me and his near-fight with Michael, and that that would account for his sudden case of lead foot....

At least until Jake said, in tones that weren't in the least drowsy, "I can't slow down. The brakes... the brakes aren't working."

This sounded interesting. I leaned forward. I guess I thought Jake was trying to scare us.

Then I saw the speed with which we were approaching the intersection in front of the school. This was no joke. We were about to plunge into four lanes of heavy traffic.

"Get out!" Jake yelled at us.

At first I didn't know what he meant. Then I saw Gina struggling to undo her seatbelt, and I knew.

But it was too late. We had already started down the dip that led past the gates, and onto the highway. If we jumped now, we'd be as dead as we were going to be the minute we plunged into those four lanes of oncoming traffic. At least if we stayed in the car, we'd have the questionable protection of the Rambler's steel walls around us—

Jake leaned on the horn, swearing loudly. Gina covered her eyes. Doc flung his arms around me, burying his face in my lap, and Dopey, to my great surprise, began to scream like a girl, very close to my ear....

Then we were sailing down the hill, speeding past a very surprised woman in a Volvo station wagon and then a stunned-looking Japanese couple in a Mercedes, both of whom managed to slam on their brakes just in time to keep from barreling into us.

We weren't so lucky with the traffic in the far two lanes, however. As we went flying across the highway, a tractor trailer with the words *Tom Cat* emblazoned on the front grid came bearing down on us, its horn blaring. The words *Tom Cat* loomed closer and closer, until suddenly I couldn't see them anymore because they were above the roof of the car....

It was at that point that I closed my eyes, so I wasn't sure if the impact I felt was in my head because I'd been expecting it so strongly, or if we'd really been struck. But the jolt was enough to send my neck snapping back the way it did on rollercoasters when the traincar suddenly took a violent ninety-degree turn.

When I opened my eyes again, however, I started to suspect the jolt hadn't been in my head since everything was spinning around, the way it does when you go on one of those teacup rides. Only we weren't on a ride. We were still in the Rambler, which was spinning across the highway like a top.

Until suddenly, with another sickening crunch, a loud crash of glass, and another very big jolt, it stopped.

And when the smoke and dust settled, we saw that we were sitting halfway in and halfway out of the Carmel-by-the-Sea Tourist Information Bureau, with a sign that said *Welcome to Carmel!* pressed up against the windshield.

CHAPTER 16

"They killed my car."

That was all Sleepy seemed capable of saying. He had been saying it ever since we'd crawled from the wreckage of what had once been the Rambler.

"My car. They killed my car."

Never mind that it hadn't actually been Sleepy's car. It had been the family car, or at any rate, the kids' car.

And never mind that Sleepy did not seem capable of telling us who this mysterious "they" was, the "they" he suspected of murdering his automobile.

He just kept saying it over and over again. And the thing was, the more he said it, the more the horror of it all sank in.

Because, of course, it wasn't the *car* someone had tried to kill. Oh, no. It was the people *in* the car that had been the intended victims.

Or, to be more accurate, one person. Me.

I really don't think I'm being at all vain. I honestly

do think that it was because of me that the Rambler's brake line was clipped. Yes, it had been clipped, so all the brake fluid had eventually leaked out. The car, being older, even, than my mother—though not quite as old as Father D—did have only the single brake line, making it vulnerable to just that sort of attack.

Let me see now, who do I know who might like to see me perish in a fiery blaze.... Oh, hang on, I know. How about Josh Saunders, Carrie Whitman, Mark Pulsford, and Felicia Bruce?

Give that girl a prize.

I couldn't, of course, tell anyone what I suspected. Not the police who showed up and took the accident report. Not the EMS guys who couldn't believe that, beyond a few bruises, none of us were seriously hurt. Not the guys from Triple A who came to tow what was left of the Rambler away. Not Michael who, having left the parking lot just moments before us, had heard the commotion and turned back, and had been one of the first to try to help us out of the car.

And certainly not my mother and stepfather, who showed up at the hospital looking tight lipped and pale faced, and kept saying things like, "It's a wonder none of you were hurt," and, "From now on, you're only driving the Land Rover."

Which caused Dopey, anyway, to brighten up. The Land Rover was way roomier than the Rambler had ever been. I suppose he figured he wouldn't have as much trouble getting horizontal with Debbie Mancuso in the Land Rover.

"I just can't understand it," my mother said, much later, after the X-rays and eye tests and poking and prodding were over, and the hospital personnel had finally let us go home. We sat in the dining room of Peninsula Pizza, the place Sleepy worked, which also happened to be one of the only places in Carmel you could get a table for six—seven, if you counted Gina—without a reservation. We must have looked, to an outsider, like one big, happy family (well, except for Gina, who sort of stuck out, though not as much as you might think) celebrating something, like a soccer game victory.

Only we knew that what we were celebrating was the fact that we were all still alive.

"I mean, it must be a miracle," my mother went on. "The doctors certainly think so. That none of you were more seriously hurt, I mean."

Doc showed her his elbow, which he'd scraped on a piece of glass while slithering out of the car after it had come to a standstill. "This could prove to be a very dangerous wound," he said, in a wounded little boy voice, "if it happens to become infected."

"Oh, sweetie." My mother reached out and stroked his hair. "I know. You were so brave when they put in those stitches."

The rest of us rolled our eyes. Doc had been playing up the injury thing all night. But it was making both him and my mother happy. She'd tried that hair-stroking thing with me, and I'd nearly broken my arm trying to get away.

"It wasn't a miracle," Andy said, shaking his head, "but simple dumb luck that you weren't all killed."

"Dumb luck nothing," Sleepy said. "My superlative driving skills are what saved us."

I hated to admit it, but Sleepy was right. (And

where did he learn a word like *superlative?* Had he been studying for his SATs behind my back?) Except for the part where we'd crashed through the plate glass window, he'd driven that tank of a car—brakeless—like an Indy 500 pro. I guess I could sort of see why Gina wouldn't let go of his arm, and kept looking up at him in this worshipful way.

Out of my newfound respect for Sleepy, I didn't even look to see what he and Gina were doing in the back of the Land Rover on the way home.

But Dopey sure did. And whatever he saw back there put him in as foul a mood as I'd ever seen him.

His stomping around and turning up of Marilyn Manson in his room only served to annoy his father, however, who went from grateful humbleness over how close he'd come to losing his "boys—and you, Suze. Oh, and Gina, too," to apoplectic rage upon hearing what he termed "that noxious mind-poison."

Alone in my room—Gina had disappeared to parts of the house unknown; well, okay, I knew where she was, I just didn't want to think about it—I did not mind the noise level in the hallway outside my door. It would keep, I realized, anybody from overhearing the very unpleasant conversation I was about to have.

"Jesse!" I called, switching on my bedroom lights and looking around for him. But both he and Spike were MIA. "Jesse, where are you? I need you."

Ghosts aren't dogs. They won't come when you call them. At least, they never used to. Not for me, anyway. Only lately—and this was something I hadn't exactly talked over with Father Dom. It was a little too weird to think about, if you asked me—the ghosts I knew had been popping up at the merest suggestion of them in my mind. Seriously. It seemed all I had to do was think about my dad, for instance, and poof, there he was.

Needless to say, this was quite embarrassing when I happened to be thinking about him while I was in the shower washing my hair, or whatever.

I kind of wondered if this had something to do with my mediator powers getting stronger with age. But if that were true, then it would stand to reason that Father Dom would be a way better mediator than me.

Only he wasn't. Different, but not better. Certainly not stronger. He couldn't summon a spirit with a single thought.

At least, I didn't think so.

Anyway, so even though ghosts don't come when you call them, Jesse always seemed to lately. He appeared before me with a shimmer, and then stood staring at me like I'd just stepped off the set of *Hellraiser III* in full costume. But may I say that I did not look half so disheveled as I felt?

"*Nombre de Dios*, Susannah," he said, paling visibly (well, for a guy who was already dead, anyway). "What happened to you?"

I looked down at myself. All right, so my blouse was torn and dirty, and my thigh-highs had sort of lost their stick. At least my hair had that all-important windswept look.

"As if you didn't know," I said sourly, sitting down on my bed and slipping out of my shoes. "I thought you said you'd babysit them all day, until Father D and I had a chance to work on Michael."

"Babysit?" Jesse knit his dark brows, revealing that he was unfamiliar with the word. "I stayed with the Angels all day, if that's what you mean."

"Oh, right," I said. "What are you saying? You went with them on their little field trip to the school parking lot to clip the Rambler's brake line?"

Jesse sat down next to me on the bed.

"Susannah." His dark-eyed gaze was riveted to my face. "Did something happen today?"

"You better believe it." I told him what had gone down, though my explanation of exactly what had been done to the car was a little sketchy given my complete ignorance of all things mechanical, and Jesse's particular lack of knowledge about the workings of the automobile. Back when he'd been alive, of course, horse and buggy had been the only way to go.

When I was through, he shook his head.

"But, Susannah," he said, "it could not have been Josh and the others. As I told you, I was with them all day. I only left them now because you called to me. They could not possibly have done what you are describing. I would have seen, and stopped them."

I blinked at him. "But if it wasn't Josh and those guys, then who could it have been? I mean, no one else wants me dead. At least, not at the moment."

Jesse continued to stare down at me. "Are you so sure you were the intended victim, Susannah?"

"Well, of course it was me." I know it sounds weird, but I was almost offended at the idea that there might be someone else on the planet worthier of murdering than myself. I must say, I do pride myself on the number of enemies I've acquired. In the mediator business, I've always considered it a sign that things were going well if there were a bunch of people who wanted me dead.

"I mean, who else but me?" I gave a laugh. "What, you think somebody's out to get *Doc?*"

Jesse, however, did not laugh.

"Think, Susannah," he urged me. "Isn't there anyone else who was in that car that someone might want to see badly hurt, or even dead?"

I narrowed my eyes at him. "You know something," I said flatly.

"No." Jesse shook his head. "But—"

"But what? God, I hate when you do the cryptic warning thing. Just tell me."

"No." He shook his head quickly. "Think, Susannah."

I sighed. There was no arguing with him when he got this way. You couldn't really blame him, I guess, for wanting to play Mr. Miyagi to my Karate Kid. It wasn't like he had a whole lot of other stuff to do.

I exhaled gustily enough to send my bangs fluttering.

"Okay," I said. "People who might not be too happy with someone—besides me—in that car. Let me see." I brightened up. "Debbie and Kelly aren't too happy about Gina. They had a nasty little interlude in the girls' room just before it happened. The car thing, I mean."

Then I frowned. "But I hardly think those two would clip a brake line to get her out of the way. In the first place, I doubt they even know what a brake line is, or where to find it. And in the second place, they might mess themselves up climbing under a car. You know, break a nail, or get oil in their hair, or whatever. Debbie probably wouldn't mind, but Kelly? Forget it. Plus they had to know they might end up killing Dopey and Sleepy, and they wouldn't want that."

"Of course not," Jesse said mildly.

It was the very tonelessness with which he uttered the words that cued me in.

"Dopey?" I shot him an incredulous look. "Who'd want Dopey dead? Or Sleepy, for that matter? I mean, those guys are so...dumb."

"Hasn't either of them," Jesse asked in that same toneless manner, "done anything that might make someone angry?"

"Well, sure," I said. "Not Sleepy so much, but Dopey? He's always doing asinine stuff like grabbing people in headlocks and throwing their books everywhere...." My voice trailed off.

Then I shook my head. "No," I said. "That's impossible."

Jesse only looked at me. "Is it?" he said.

"No, you don't understand." I stood up and started pacing my room. At some point during our conversation, Spike had slunk through the window. Now he sat on the floor at Jesse's feet, vigorously lashing himself with his sandpapery tongue.

"I mean, he was there," I explained. "Michael was there, right after it happened. He helped us out of the car. He..." My last sight of Michael that evening had been just as the ambulance doors closed on me and Gina and Sleepy and Dopey and Doc. Michael's face had been pale—even more than usual—and concerned.

No. "That just..." I got as far as Gina's daybed before I spun around to face Jesse again. "That just can't be," I said. "Michael would never do something like that."

Jesse laughed. There was no humor in the sound, however.

"Wouldn't he?" he wanted to know. "I can think of four people who might have a very different opinion on the matter."

"But *why* would he do it?" I shook my head again, emphatically enough to send the ends of my hair flying. "I mean, Dopey's a butthead, it's true, but enough of one so that someone might feel compelled to *murder* him? Not to mention a bunch of innocent people along with him? Including *me?*" I raised my indignant gaze from the sight of Spike chewing on his own foot, trying to get the grime out from between his toes. "Michael couldn't possibly want to see *me* dead. I'm the best chance he's got for a date to the prom!"

Jesse didn't say anything. And in the silence, I remembered something. And what I remembered took my breath away.

"Oh, God," I said, and, clutching my chest, I sank down onto the daybed.

Jesse's neutral expression sharpened into one of concern.

"What is it, Susannah?" he asked worriedly. "Are you ill?"

I nodded. "Oh, yeah," I said, staring unseeingly at the wall across from me. "I think I'm going to be sick. Jesse...he asked me if I wanted to ride with him. Right before it happened. He was *insistent* I ride with him. In fact, when Sleepy said I had to go with him or he'd tell Mom, I thought the two of them were going to get into a fist-fight."

"Of course," Jesse said in what was, for him, a very dry tone. "His—what did you call it? Oh, yes—date for the prom was about to be exterminated."

"Oh, God!" I stood up and started pacing again. "Oh, God, why? Why *Dopey?* I mean, he's a jerk and all, but why would Michael want to *kill* him?"

Jesse said, quietly, "Perhaps for the same reason he killed Josh and the others."

I stopped dead in my tracks. Slowly, I turned my head to look at him. But I didn't see him. Not really. I was remembering something Dopey had said—weeks ago, it seemed like, but it had actually only been a night or two before. We'd been talking about the accident that had killed the RLS Angels, and Dopey had said something about Mark Pulsford. "We happen to have partied together," he'd said. "Last month, in the Valley."

At the same party in the Valley, I wondered, my blood suddenly running cold, where Lila Meducci had fallen into the pool?

A second later, without another word to Jesse, I'd ripped open the door to my room, taken the three strides across the hall to Dopey's room, and was banging on the door with all my might.

"Chill!" Dopey thundered from inside. "I turned it down already!"

"It's not about the music," I said. "It's about something else. Can I come in?"

I heard the sound of barbells falling back into their stand. Then Dopey grunted, "Yeah. I guess so."

I laid my hand on the knob and turned it.

I'd like to point out something here. I have been in Doc's room. Many times, in fact, as he is always the stepbrother I go to when I have a homework problem I cannot solve, in spite of the fact that he is three grades behind me. And I have even been in Sleepy's room since he usually needs actual physical shaking in order to wake him up in the morning in time to drive us all to school.

But I had never, ever been in Dopey's room before. Truth be told, I had always hoped I might never have a reason to cross that particular threshold.

Now, however, I had a reason. I took a deep breath and went in.

It was dark. This was because of Dopey's decision to paint three of his walls purple and one white, Mission Academy wrestling team colors. He had chosen a purple so dark it was almost black. The darkness of those three walls was only alleviated by the occasional poster of Michael Jordan urging the viewer to Just Do It.

The floor of Dopey's room was a deep carpet of dirty socks and underwear. The odor was pungent—a mixture of sweat and baby powder. Not unpleasant, necessarily, but not an odor *I'd* particularly want permeating my wardrobe. Dopey, however, did not seem to mind.

"Well?" He was stretched out on his back on a padded bench. Above his chest hung a set of barbells. I would not have liked to hazard a guess as to how much weight he was lifting, but allow me to assure you, with enough reps, I was quite sure he'd have no trouble heaving Debbie Mancuso out the window in the event of a fire. Which is all a girl really needs out of a boyfriend, if you ask me.

"Dope—" I took another deep breath. What was with the baby powder? Wait. Don't tell me. I don't want to know. "Brad. Were you at that party in the Valley where Lila Meducci fell into the pool?"

Dopey had reached up and seized the barbell. Now he heaved it into the air, awarding me a glimpse of his excessively hairy armpits. I tried not to hurl at the sight of them.

"What are you talking about?" he grunted.

"Lila Meducci."

Dopey had lowered the barbell until it was just above his chest. His biceps had bunched up into melon-sized balls. Allow me to point out that normally, the sight of a male bicep that size would have caused my knees to go weak. But then, these biceps were Dopey's, so all I could do was swallow hard and hope the slices of pepperoni pizza I'd downed for dinner would stay where they were.

"Michael's little sister," I elaborated. "She nearly drowned at a party out in the Valley last month. I was wondering if it was the same party you mentioned you'd been to, the one where you'd run into Mark Pulsford."

Up went the barbells.

"Could have been," Dopey said. "I don't know. Why do you care?"

"Brad," I said. "It's important. I mean, if you were there, I think you would know. An ambulance must have shown up."

"I guess," he said between reps. "I mean, I was pretty wasted."

"You *guess* that a girl almost drowned in front of you?" I don't have much patience for Dopey under the best of circumstances. In this particular case, my tolerance for his stupidity had dipped to an all-time low.

Dopey let the barbell fall back into its stand with a clatter. Then he sat up and regarded me testily.

"Look," he said. "If I tell you I was there, what are you going to do? Go running to Mom and Dad, right? So why would I tell you? I mean, seriously, Suze. Why would I?"

Aside from my great surprise at hearing Dopey, too, mess up and call my mother *Mom,* I was prepared for the question.

"I won't tell," I said. "I swear I won't tell, Brad. Only I have to know."

He still looked suspicious. "Why? So you can tell that creepy albino friend of yours, and she can put it in the school paper? 'Brad Ackerman stood there like a schmo while a girl almost died.' Is that it?"

"I swear it isn't," I said.

He shrugged his heavy shoulders. "Fine," he said. "You know what? I don't even care. It's not like my life doesn't already suck. I mean, I haven't got a hope of getting down to one-sixty-eight before sectionals, and it's pretty clear now that your friend Gina likes Jake better 'n me." He eyed me. "Doesn't she?"

I shifted my weight uncomfortably. "I don't know," I said. "I think she likes both of you."

"Yeah," Dopey said sarcastically. "That's why

she's in here right now with me instead of locked in with Jake, doing whatever."

"I'm sure they're just talking," I said.

"Right." Dopey shook his head. I was a bit stunned. I had never seen him looking so... human. Nor had I known he had goals. What was this 168 business? And did he really care that much about Gina that he would think his life sucked just because he didn't think she liked him back?

Weird. Really weird stuff.

"You want to know about that party in the Valley?" he asked. "I was there. All right? Are you happy now? I was there. Like I said, I was wasted. I didn't see her fall in. I only noticed her as somebody was pulling her out." Again, he shook his head. "That was really uncool, you know? I mean, she shouldn't have been there in the first place. Nobody invited her. If you can't hold your liquor, you got no business drinking, you know? But some of these girls, they'll do just about anything to get in with us."

I knit my eyebrows. "Us?"

He looked at me like I was stupid. "You know," he said. "The jocks. The popular people. Meducci's sister—I didn't know it was her until your mom said it the other night at the dinner table—she was one of those girls. Always hanging around, trying to get one of us guys from the team to ask her out. So she could be popular, too, see?"

I saw. Suddenly, I saw only too well.

Which was why I left Dopey's room then without another word. What was there to say? I knew what I had to do. I guess I had known it all along. I just hadn't wanted to admit it.

But now I knew. Like Michael Meducci, I thought I had no other choice.

And like Michael Meducci, I needed to be stopped. Only I didn't think so. Not then.

Just like Michael.

CHAPTER 17

Gina was in my room when I came back from my visit to Dopey. Both Jesse and Spike, however, were gone. Which was actually fine by me.

"Hey," Gina said, looking up from the toenail she'd been painting. "Where have you been?"

I strode past her and started wriggling out of my school clothes. "Dopey's room," I said. "Look, cover for me, will you?" I stepped into a pair of jeans, then started lacing up my Timberland boots. "I'm going to be out for a while. Just tell them I'm in the bathtub. It would help if you let the water run. Tell them it's cramps again."

"They're going to start thinking you've got endometriosis, or something." Gina watched as I tugged a black turtleneck sweater over my head. "Where are you really going?"

"Out," I said. I pulled on the windbreaker I'd worn the other night to the beach. This time I tucked a hat into my pocket, along with the gloves.

"Oh, sure. Out." Gina shook her head, looking concerned. "Suze, are you all right?"

"Of course I am. Why?"

"You've got kind of...well, a crazy look in your eye."

"I'm fine," I said. "I figured it out, is all."

"Figured what out?" Gina put the cap on her nail polish and stood up. "Suze, what are you talking about?"

"What happened today." I climbed up onto the window seat. "With the brake line. Michael did it."

"Michael *Meducci?*" Gina looked at me as if I were nuts. "Suze, are you sure?"

"Sure as I'm standing here talking to you."

"But why? Why would he do that? I thought he was in love with you."

"With me, maybe," I said with a shrug as I pushed the window open wider. "But he's got a pretty big grudge against Brad."

"Brad? What did Brad ever do to Michael Meducci?"

"Stand around," I said, "and let his little sister die. Well, almost, anyway. I'm out of here, okay, Gina? I'll explain everything when I get back."

And then I slipped through the window, and climbed down to the porch roof. Outside, it was dark and cool and silent, except for the chirp of crickets and the far-off sound of the waves hitting the beach. Or was that the traffic down on the highway? I couldn't tell. After listening for a minute to make sure no one downstairs had heard me, I walked down the sloping roof to the gutter, where I squatted, ready to jump, knowing the pine needles below would cushion my landing.

"Suze!" A shadow blocked out the light streaming from the bay windows to my room.

I looked back over my shoulder. Gina was leaning out, looking anxiously after me.

"Shouldn't we—" She sounded, I noted in some distant part of my mind, frightened. "I mean, shouldn't we call the police? If this stuff about Michael is true—"

I stared at her as if she'd suggested I... well, jump off the Golden Gate Bridge.

"The *police?*" I echoed. "No way. This is between Michael and me."

"Suze—" Gina shook her head so that her springy curls bounced. "This is serious stuff. I mean, this guy is a murderer. I really think we need to call in the professionals here—"

"I am a professional," I said, offended. "I'm a mediator, remember?"

Gina did not look comforted by this piece of information.

"But... well, what are you going to *do,* Suze?"

I smiled at her reassuringly.

"Oh," I said. "That's easy. I'm going to show him what happens when somebody tries to kill someone I care about."

And then I leaped off of the roof into the darkness.

I couldn't bring myself to take the Land Rover. Oh, sure, I was perfectly willing to commit what pretty much amounted to murder, but drive without a license? No way! Instead, I hauled out one of the many ten speeds Andy had tucked away along the carport wall. A few seconds later, I was flying down the hill from our house, tears streaming from my eyes. Not because I was crying, or anything, but because the wind was so cold on my face as I sailed down into the Valley.

I called Michael from a pay phone outside the Safeway. An older woman—his mother, I suppose—answered. I asked if I could speak to Michael. She said, "Yes, of course," in that pleased way mothers use when their child gets his or her first call from a member of the opposite sex. And I would know. My mother uses that voice every time a boy calls me and she answers. You can't really blame her. It happens so rarely.

Mrs. Meducci must have tipped Michael off that it was a girl, since his voice sounded much deeper than usual when he said hello.

"Michael?" I said, just to be sure it was him and not his father.

"Suze?" he said in his normal voice. "Oh, my God, Suze, I'm so glad it's you. Did you get my message? I must have called about ten times. I followed the ambulance to the hospital, but they wouldn't let me into the emergency room to see you. Only if you were admitted, they said. Which you weren't, right?"

"Nope," I said. "Fit as a fiddle."

"Thank God. Oh, Suze, you don't have any idea how scared I was when I heard that crash and realized it was you—"

"Yeah," I said shortly. "It was scary. Listen, Michael, I'm in a jam of a different kind, and I was wondering if you could help me out."

Michael said, "You know I'd do anything for you, Suze."

Yeah. Like try to kill my stepbrothers and my best friend.

"I'm stranded," I said. "At the Safeway. It's kind of a long story. I was wondering if there was any possible way—"

"I'll be there," Michael said, "in three minutes." Then he hung up.

He was there in two. I'd barely had time to stash the bike between a couple of Dumpsters in the back of the store before I saw him pull up in his green rental sedan, peering into the brightly lit windows of the supermarket as if he expected to see me inside riding the stupid mechanical rocking horse, or whatever. I approached the car from the parking lot, then leaned over to tap on the passenger side window.

Michael whipped around, startled by the sound. When he saw it was me, his face—pastier than ever in the fluorescent lights—relaxed. He leaned over and opened the door.

"Hop in," he said cheerfully. "Boy, you don't know how glad I am to see you in one piece."

"Yeah?" I slid into the front passenger seat, then slammed the door closed after I'd tucked my feet in. "Well, me too. Happy to be in one piece, I mean. Ha ha."

"Ha ha." Michael's laugh, rather than being sarcastic, as mine had been, was nervous. Or at least I chose to think so.

"Well," he said as we sat there in front of the supermarket, the motor running. "You want me to take you, um, home?"

"No." I turned my head to look at him.

You might be wondering what I was thinking at a

moment like that. I mean, what goes through a person's head when they know they're about to do something that could result in another person's death?

Well, I'll tell you. Not a whole heck of a lot. I was thinking that Michael's rental car smelled funny. I was wondering if the last person who had used it had spilled cologne in it, or something.

Then I realized the smell of cologne was coming from Michael himself. He had apparently splashed on a little Carolina Herrera For Men before coming to get me. How flattering.

"I have an idea," I said, as if I had only just then thought of it. "Let's go to the Point."

Michael's hands fell off the steering wheel. He hurried to right them, placing them at two and four o'clock, like the good driver he was.

"I beg your pardon?" he said.

"The Point." I thought maybe I wasn't being alluring enough, or something. So I reached over and laid a hand on his arm. He was wearing a suede jacket. Beneath my fingertips, the suede felt very soft, and beneath the suede, Michael's bicep was as hard and as round as Dopey's had looked.

"You know," I said. "For the view. It's a beautiful night."

Michael wasted no more time. He put the car in gear and began pulling out from the parking lot before I even had time to remove my hand.

"Great," he said. His voice was maybe a little uneven, so he cleared his throat, and said, with a little more dignity, "I mean, that sounds all right."

A few seconds later, we were cruising along the

Pacific Coast Highway. It was only ten o'clock or so, but there weren't many other cars on the road. It was, after all, a weeknight. I wondered if Michael's mother, before he'd left the house, had told him to be home at a certain time. I wondered if, when he didn't come home by curfew, she'd worry. How long, I wondered, would she wait before calling the police? The hospital emergency rooms?

"So nobody," Michael said as he drove, "was really hurt, right? In the accident?"

"No," I replied. "No one was hurt."

"That's good," Michael said.

"Is it?" I pretended to be looking out the passenger side window. But really I was watching Michael's reflection.

"What do you mean?" he asked quickly.

I shrugged. "I don't know," I said. "It's just that...well, you know. Brad."

"Oh." He gave a little chuckle. There wasn't any real humor in it, though. "Yeah. Brad."

"I mean, I try to get along with him," I said. "But it's so hard. Because he can be such a jerk sometimes."

"I can imagine," Michael said. Pretty mildly, I thought.

I turned in my seat so that I was almost facing him.

"Like, you know what he said tonight?" I asked. Without waiting for a reply, I said, "He told me he was at that party. The one where your sister fell. You know. Into the pool."

I do not think it was my imagination that Michael's grip on the wheel tightened. "Really?"

"Yeah. You should have heard what he said about it, too."

Michael's face, in profile to mine, looked grim. "What did he say?"

I toyed with the seatbelt I'd fastened around myself. "No," I said. "I shouldn't tell you."

"No, really," Michael said. "I'd like to know."

"It's so mean, though," I said.

"Tell me what he said." Michael's voice was very calm.

"Well," I said. "All right. He basically said—and he wasn't quite as succinct as this, because, as you know, he's pretty much incapable of forming complete sentences—but basically he said your sister got what she deserved because she shouldn't have been at that party in the first place. He said she hadn't been invited. Only popular people were supposed to be there. Can you believe that?"

Michael carefully passed a pickup truck. "Yes," he said quietly. "Actually, I can."

"I mean, popular people. He actually said that. Popular people." I shook my head. "And what defines popular? That's what I'd like to know. I mean, your sister was unpopular why? Because she wasn't a jock? She wasn't a cheerleader? She didn't have the right clothes? What?"

"All of those things," Michael said in the same quiet voice.

"As if any of that *matters*," I said. "As if being intelligent and compassionate and kind to others doesn't count for anything. No, all that matters is whether you're friends with the right people."

"Unfortunately," Michael said, "that oftentimes appears to be the case."

"Well," I said. "I think it's crap. I said so, too. To

Brad. I was like, 'So all of you just stood there while this girl nearly died because no one invited her in the first place?' He denied it, of course. But you know it's true."

"Yes," Michael said. We were driving along Big Sur now, the road narrowing while, at the same time, growing darker. "I do, actually. If my sister had been... well, Kelly Prescott, for instance, someone would have pulled her out at once, rather than stand there laughing at her as she drowned."

It was hard to see his expression since there was no moon. The only light there was to see by was the glow from the console in the dashboard. Michael looked sickly in it, and not just because the light had a greenish tinge to it.

"Is that what happened?" I asked him. "Did people do that? Laugh at her while she was drowning?"

He nodded. "That's what one of the EMS guys told the police. Everybody thought she was faking it." He let out a humorless laugh. "My sister—that was all she wanted, you know? To be popular. To be like them. And they stood there. They all just stood there laughing while she drowned."

I said, "Well. I heard everyone was pretty drunk." Including your sister, I thought, but didn't say out loud.

"That's no excuse," Michael said. "But of course nobody did anything about it. The girl who had the party—her parents got a fine. That's all. My sister may never wake up, and all they got was a fine."

We had reached, I saw, the turn-off to the observation point. Michael honked before he went around the corner. No one was on the other side. He swung neatly into a parking space, but he didn't switch off the ignition. Instead, he sat there, staring out into the inky blackness that was the sea and sky.

I was the one who reached over and turned the motor off. The dashboard light went off a second later, plunging us into absolute darkness.

"So," I said. The silence in the car was pretty deafening. There were no cars on the road behind us. If I opened the window, I knew the sounds of the wind and waves would come rushing in. Instead, I just sat there.

Slowly, the darkness outside the car became less consummate. As my eyes adjusted to it, I could even make out the horizon where the black sky met the even blacker sea.

Michael turned his head. "It was Carrie Whitman," he said. "The girl who had the party."

I nodded, not taking my gaze off the horizon. "I know."

"Carrie Whitman," he said again. "Carrie Whitman was in that car. The one that went off the cliff last Saturday night."

"You mean," I said quietly, "the car you pushed off the cliff last Saturday night."

Michael's head didn't move. I looked at him, but I couldn't quite read his expression.

But I could hear the resignation in his voice.

"You know," he said. It was a statement, not a question. "I thought you might."

"After today, you mean?" I reached down and undid my seatbelt. "When you nearly killed me?"

"I'm so sorry." He lowered his head, and finally, I

could see his eyes. They were filled with tears. "Suze, I don't know how I'll ever—"

"There was no seminar on extraterrestrial life at that institute, was there?" I glared at him. "Last Saturday night, I mean. You came out here, and you loosened the bolts on that guardrail. Then you sat and waited for them. You knew they'd come here after the dance. You knew they'd come, and you waited. And when you heard that stupid horn, you rammed them. You pushed them over the side of that cliff. And you did it in cold blood."

Michael did something surprising then. He reached out and touched my hair where it curled out from beneath the knit watch cap I was wearing.

"I knew you'd understand," he said. "From the moment I saw you, I knew you, out of all of them, were the only one who'd understand."

I seriously wanted to throw up. I mean it. He didn't get it. He so didn't get it. I mean, hadn't he thought about his mother at all? His poor mother, who had been so excited because a girl had called him? His mother, who already had one kid in the hospital? Hadn't he thought how his mother was going to feel when it came out that her only son was a murderer? Hadn't he thought about that *at all?*

Maybe he had. Maybe he had, and he thought she'd be glad. Because he'd avenged what had happened to his sister. Well, almost, anyway. There were still a few loose ends in the form of Brad...and everyone else who'd been at that party, I suppose. I mean, why just stop at Brad? I wondered how he'd managed to secure the guest list, and if he intended to kill everyone on it or just a select few.

"How did you know, anyway?" he asked in what I suppose he meant to be this tender voice. But all it did was make me want to throw up even more. "About the guardrail, I mean? And their car horn. That wasn't in the papers."

"How did I know?" I jerked my head from his reach. "They told me."

He looked a little hurt at my pulling away from him. "*They* told you? Who do you mean?"

"Carrie," I said. "And Josh and Felicia and Mark. The kids you killed."

His hurt look changed. It went from confused, to startled, and then to cynical, all in a matter of seconds.

"Oh," he said with a little laugh. "Right. The ghosts. You tried to warn me about them before, didn't you? Right here, as a matter of fact."

I just looked at him. "Laugh all you want," I said. "But the fact is, Michael, they've been wanting to kill you for a while now. And after the stunt you pulled today with the Rambler, I am seriously thinking about letting them."

He stopped laughing. "Suze," he said. "Your strange fixation with the spirit world aside, I told you: today was an accident. You weren't supposed to be in that car. You were supposed to ride home with me. Brad was the one. Brad was the one I wanted dead, not you."

"And what about David?" I demanded. "My little brother? He's twelve years old, Michael. He was in that car. Did you want him dead, too? And Jake? He was probably delivering pizzas the night your sister was hurt. Should he die for what happened to her?

Or my friend Gina? I guess she deserves to die, too, even though she's never even been to a party in the Valley."

Michael's face was white against the bits of sky I could see through the window behind his head.

"I didn't mean for anyone to get hurt," he said, in an oddly toneless voice. "Anybody except for the guilty, I mean."

"Well, you didn't do a very good job," I said. "In fact, you did a lousy job. You really messed up. And do you know why?"

I saw his eyelids, behind his glasses, narrow.

"I think I'm starting to," he said.

"Because you tried to kill some people I happen to care about." I swallowed. Something hard, that hurt, was growing in my throat. "And that's why, Michael, it's going to stop. Right here. Right now."

He continued to stare at me though those narrowed eyelids.

"Oh," he said in the same expressionless voice. "It's going to stop, all right. Believe me."

I knew what he was driving at. I almost laughed. If it hadn't been for the painful lump in my throat, I would have.

"Michael," I said. "Don't even try. You so don't know who you're messing with."

"No," Michael said quietly. "I guess I don't, do I? I thought you were different. I thought you, out of everyone at school, would be able to see things from my point of view. But I can see now that you're just like everybody else."

"You don't have any idea," I said, "how much I wish I were."

"I'm sorry, Suze," Michael said, undoing his own seatbelt. "I really thought you and I could be...well, friends, anyway. But I am getting the distinct impression that you don't approve of what I've been doing. Even though no one—*no one*—will miss those people. They really were wastes of space, Suze. They had nothing meaningful to contribute. I mean, look at Brad. Would it be such a tragedy if he simply ceased to exist?"

"It would," I said, "to his father."

Michael shrugged. "I suppose. Still, I think the world would be a better place without all the Josh Saunderses and Brad Ackermans." He smiled at me. There was nothing, however, warm in that smile. "You, however, disagree, I can see. It even sounds to me as if you're contemplating trying to stop me. And I really can't have that."

"So what are you going to do?" I gave him a very sarcastic look. "Kill me?"

"I don't want to," he said. "Believe me."

Then he cracked his knuckles. Can I just tell you, I found this quite creepy. I mean, aside from the fact that cracking your knuckles in front of somebody is creepy, anyway, this was especially disturbing since it drew attention to the fact that Michael's hands were actually quite large, and were attached to these arms that I remembered from the beach were remarkably muscular, and filled with ropy sinews. I'm not exactly a delicate flower, but hands attached to a pair of arms like that could do a girl like me some serious damage.

"But I guess," Michael said, "you haven't left me with much choice, have you?"

Oh, sure. Blame the victim, why don't you?

I don't know if I said the words aloud, or simply thought them. I only know I went, "Now would be a good time for Josh and his friends to show up," and that a second later Josh Saunders, Carrie Whitman, Mark Pulsford, and Felicia Bruce all appeared, standing in the gravel by the passenger side door of Michael's rental car.

They stood there blinking for a second, as if unsure what had happened. Then they looked beyond me, at the boy behind the steering wheel.

And that's when all hell broke loose.

CHAPTER

18

Was it what I intended to happen all along?

I don't know. Certainly there'd been a moment in Dopey's room when I'd been seized by a kind of rage. It was rage, not bicycle pedals, that had propelled me down into the Valley, and rage that had prompted me to put that quarter into that pay phone and call Michael.

Some of that rage, however, dissipated when I spoke to Michael's mother. Yes, he was a murderer. Yes, he'd tried to kill me and a number of people I cared about.

But he had a mother. A mother who loved him enough to be excited because a girl was calling him, maybe for the first time in his life.

Still, I got into that car with him. I told him to drive to the Point, even though I knew what was there waiting for him. And I got him to admit it. All of it. Out loud.

And then I called them. There was no doubt

about that. I called the RLS Angels. And when they showed up, all I did was calmly get out of the car.

That's right. I got out of the way. And I let them do what they'd been wanting to do for so long... since the night of their deaths, actually.

Look, I'm not proud of it. And I can't say that I stood there and watched it with any relish. When the seatbelt Michael had removed suddenly wrapped around his throat, and his adjustable car seat started creeping inexorably toward the steering wheel, crushing his legs, I didn't feel good about it.

The Angels sure seemed to, however.

And they probably should have. Their telekinetic powers, I could see, had come a long way. They weren't messing around with any seaweed ropes or mardi gras decorations now. The force of their combined power was strong enough to have flicked on the rental car's lights and windshield wipers. Through the rolled up windows, I could hear the radio blare to life. Britney Spears was bemoaning her latest heartache as Michael Meducci clawed at the seatbelt around his neck. The car had begun to rock, and was lit eerily from inside, almost as if the dashboard lights were halogens that someone had set on bright.

And all the while, the RLS Angels stood there in eerie silence, their hands stretched out toward the car, and their gazes fixed on Michael. I mean, even for ghosts they looked spooky, glowing in that unearthly way, the girls in their long dresses and wrist corsages, and the boys in their tuxes. I shuddered, watching them, and it wasn't just from the cold breeze coming off the ocean, either.

I hate to say it, but it was Britney that broke the spell for me. I mean, she's likable enough, but to have to die while listening to her? I don't know. It just seemed a bit harsh, somehow.

And then there was poor Mrs. Meducci. She had already lost one child—well, more or less. Could I really just stand there and watch her lose another?

Minutes—maybe even seconds—before, the answer to that question might have been yes. But when it came down to it, I just couldn't. I couldn't, in spite of what Michael had done. I simply had too many years of mediation behind me. Too many years, and too many deaths. I couldn't stand there and allow yet another one to occur right before my eyes.

Michael's face was contorted and purple, his glasses askew, when I finally shouted, *"Stop!"*

Instantly, the car stopped rocking. The windshield wipers stilled. Britney's voice was cut off midnote, and Michael's car seat started sliding slowly back. The seatbelt loosened around his neck enough to allow him to gasp for air. He collapsed against the back of the seat, looking confused and frightened, his chest heaving.

Josh blinked at me like someone newly wakened from a trance. "What?" he said, sounding annoyed.

I said, "I'm sorry. But I can't let you do this."

Josh and the others exchanged glances. Mark was the first to speak. He gave a little laugh and went, "Oh, *right.*"

Then the radio blared to life again, and suddenly, the car was rocking on its shocks.

I reacted swiftly and decisively by hammering a fist into Mark Pulsford's gut. This threw off the Angels' concentration enough so that Michael was able to scrape open the driver's side door and throw himself out of the car before anything else could start strangling him. He lay in the gravel, moaning.

Mark, on the other hand, recovered all too quickly from my assault.

"You bitch," he said, looking mightily offended. "What gives?"

"Yeah." Josh was clearly livid. His blue eyes were like shards of ice as they glinted at me. "First you say we can't kill him. Then you say we can. Then you say we can't. Well, guess what? We're tired of this mediation crap. We're killing him, and that's the end of it."

That was when the car started rocking with enough energy that it looked as if it was going to flip over, right on top of Michael.

"No!" I cried. "Look, I was wrong, all right? I mean, he tried to kill me, too, and I'll admit, I went a little wacko. But believe me, this isn't the way—"

"Speak for yourself," Josh said.

And a second later, I was flying backward through the air, blown off my feet by a blast of energy so strong, I was convinced Michael's car had blown up.

It wasn't until I landed hard in the dirt on the far side of the parking area that I realized it hadn't been the car exploding at all. It had merely been the combined force of the Angels' psychic power, thrown casually my way. I had been tossed aside as easily as an ant flicked off a picnic table.

I guess that's when I knew I was in some real trouble. I had, I realized, unleashed a monster. Or four of them, I should say.

I was struggling to get back up to my feet when Jesse materialized beside me, looking almost as angry as Josh.

"Nombre de Dios," I heard him breathe as he took in the sight before him. Then he looked down at me. "What is happening here?" he demanded, holding out a hand to help me up. "I turn around for one second, and they are gone. Did you call them?"

Flinching—and not from pain—I took his hand, and let him pull me up.

"Yes," I admitted, brushing myself off. "But I didn't... well, I didn't mean for *this* to happen."

Jesse looked at Michael, who was crawling across the parking lot, trying to get away from his gyrating car.

"Nombre de Dios, Susannah," Jesse said again, incredulously. "What did you expect to happen? You bring that boy *here,* of all places? And now you ask them not to kill him?" Shaking his head, Jesse started striding toward the Angels.

"You don't understand," I protested, trotting after him. "He tried to kill me. And Doc and Gina and Dopey and—"

"So you do *this?* Susannah, don't you know by now that you are not a killer?" Jesse's dark-eyed gaze bored into me. "Kindly don't try to act like one. The only person who will end up getting hurt by it is you."

I was so taken aback by the rebuke in his tone, tears filled my eyes. I mean it. Actual tears. Furious. That's what I told myself. I was crying because I was furious with him. Not because he'd hurt my feelings. Not at all.

But Jesse didn't notice my fury. He'd turned his

back on me, and now he strode up to the Angels. A second later, the car stopped rocking, the windshield wipers and radio stilled, and the lights went dead. The Angels were strong, it was true. But Jesse had been dead a lot longer than they had.

"Get back to the beach," Jesse said to them.

Josh actually laughed out loud.

"You're kidding me, right?" he said.

"I am not kidding you," Jesse said.

"No way," Mark Pulsford said.

"Yeah." Carrie pointed at me. "I mean, *she* called us. *She* said it was all right."

Jesse did not turn his head in the direction Carrie was pointing. It was pretty clear he was disgusted with me.

"Now she says it is not," Jesse informed them. "You will do as she says."

"Don't you get it?" Josh's eyes were flashing again, flashing with the psychic energy he was so filled with. "He killed us. He *killed* us."

"And he will be punished for it," Jesse said evenly. "But not by you."

"By who, then?" Josh demanded.

"By," Jesse said, "the law."

"*Bullshit!*" Josh exploded. "That is bullshit, man! We've been waiting all day for *the law!* The old man said that was what was going to happen, but I don't see this kid being taken away by any boys in blue. Do you? I don't think it's going to happen. So let us teach him a lesson *our* way."

Jesse shook his head. It was a dangerous move with four angry, out-of-control young ghosts bearing down on him. But he did it anyway.

I took a step closer to Jesse as I saw the RLS Angels shimmer with rage. I stood on tiptoe so he could hear me when I whispered, "I'll take the girls. You take the boys."

"No." Jesse's expression was grim. "Leave, Susannah. While they are occupied with me, run for the road and flag down the next automobile you see. Then go with them to safety."

Uh, yeah. Right.

"And leave you to deal with them alone?" I glared at him. "What are you, nuts?"

"Susannah," he hissed. "You don't understand. They'll kill you—"

I laughed. I actually laughed, all my anger with him gone.

Jesse was right. I didn't understand.

"Let them try," I said.

That's when they rushed us.

I guess the Angels must have agreed upon an arrangement amongst themselves that was similar to the one I'd tried to make with Jesse, since the girls came at me and both boys went for Jesse. I wasn't too dismayed. I mean, two on one is kind of unfair, but, except for the whole telekinetic power thing, I felt we were pretty even. Carrie and Felicia hadn't been fighters when they'd been alive—that much was clear from the very first moment they tackled me—so they didn't have a real solid idea of where it was best to apply a fist in order to cause the most pain.

At least, that's what I thought before they started hitting me. The thing I hadn't counted on was the fact that these girls—and their boyfriends, too—were really, really mad.

And if you think about it, they had a right to be. Okay, maybe they had been jerks when they'd been alive—they didn't exactly strike me as the kind of people I'd want to hang out with, with their obsession with partying and their elitist attitudes—but they'd been young. They would likely have grown into, if not thoughtful, then at least productive citizens.

Michael Meducci had put a stop to that, though. And they were spitting mad about it.

I guess you could argue that their own behavior hadn't exactly been above reproach. I mean, they had thrown that party where Lila Meducci had been so seriously hurt, due not only to her own stupidity, but also their—and their parents'—negligence.

But that didn't seem to occur to them. No, as far as the RLS Angels were concerned, they'd been cheated. Cheated from their lives. And somebody was going to have to pay for that.

That someone was Michael Meducci. And anyone who tried to stand in the way of their achieving that goal.

Their wrath was exquisite. Really. I don't think I've ever been as completely, one hundred percent angry as those ghosts were. Oh, I've been mad, sure. But never that mad, and never for that long.

The RLS Angels were furious. And they took that fury out on Jesse and me.

I didn't even see the first blow. It spun me around the way that semi truck had spun the Rambler. I felt my lip split. Blood flew out in a fountain from my face. Some of it landed on the girls' evening gowns.

They didn't even notice. They just hit me again.

I don't want you to think I didn't hit back. I did. I was good. Really good.

Just not good enough. I had to reassess my whole theory on that two-on-one thing. It *wasn't* fair. Felicia Bruce and Carrie Whitman were killing me.

And there wasn't a blessed thing I could do about it.

I couldn't even look over to see if Jesse was bearing up any better than I was. Every time I turned my head, it seemed, another fist connected with it. Soon I couldn't see at all. My eyes had filled up with blood, which appeared to be streaming from a cut in my forehead. Either that or some blood vessels in my eyes had burst from the force of some of those blows. I hoped Jesse, at least, would be all right. It wasn't like he could die, or anything. Not like I could. The one thing that kept going through my head was, Well, if they kill me, then I'll finally know where everybody goes. Once a mediator has sent them packing, I mean.

At one point during Felicia and Carrie's assault, I tripped over something—something that was warm and somewhat soft. I wasn't sure what it was—I couldn't see it, of course—until it moaned my name.

"Suze," it said.

At first I didn't recognize the voice. Then I realized Michael's throat must have been crushed by that seatbelt. All he could do was croak.

"Suze," he wheezed. "What's happening?"

The terror in his voice, I thought, showed that he was probably as frightened now as Josh, Carrie, Mark, and Felicia had been when he'd rammed their car and sent them plummeting to their deaths. It served him right, I thought, in some distant part of my mind that wasn't concentrating on trying to escape the blows that were raining down on me.

"Suze," Michael moaned, beneath me. "Make it stop."

As if I could. As if I had anything like control over what was happening to me. If I lived through this—which didn't seem likely—some big changes were going to be made. First and foremost, I was going to practice my kick-boxing a lot more faithfully.

And then something happened. I can't tell you what it was because, like I said, I couldn't see.

But I could hear. And what I heard was perhaps the sweetest sound I'd ever heard in my life.

It was a siren. Police or firetruck, ambulance or paramedic, I couldn't tell. But it was coming closer, and closer, and closer still, until suddenly, I could hear the vehicle's tires crunching on the gravel in front of me. The blows that had been raining down on me abruptly ceased, and I sagged against Michael, who was pushing at me feebly, saying, "The cops. Get off me. It's the cops. I gotta go."

A second later, hands were touching me. Warm hands. Not ghost hands. Human hands.

Then a man's voice was saying, "Don't worry, miss. We've got you. We've got you. Can you stand up?"

I could, but standing caused waves of pain to go shooting through me. I recognized that pain. It was the kind of pain that was so intense, it seemed ridiculous...so ridiculous, I started to giggle. Really. Because it was just funny that anything could hurt that much. It meant, pain like that, that something, somewhere, was broken.

Then something soft was pressed beneath me, and I was told to lie down. More pain—burning, searing pain that left me chuckling weakly. More hands touched me.

Then I heard a familiar voice calling my name as if from somewhere very far away.

"Susannah. Susannah, it's me, Father Dominic. Can you hear me, Susannah?"

I opened my eyes. Someone had wiped the blood from them. I could see again.

I was lying on an ambulance gurney. Red and white lights were flashing all around me. Two emergency medical technicians were messing with the wound in my scalp.

But that wasn't what hurt. My chest. Ribs. I'd cracked a few. I could tell.

Father Dominic's face loomed over my gurney. I tried to smile—tried to speak—but I couldn't. My lip was too sore to move it.

"Gina called me," Father Dominic said, I suppose in answer to the questioning look I'd given him. "She told me you were going to meet Michael. I guessed—after she told me what you'd said about the accident today—that this was where you'd bring him. Oh, Susannah, how I wish you hadn't."

"Yeah," one of the EMTs said. "Looks like he worked her over pretty good."

"Hey." His partner was grinning. "Who you kidding? She gave as good as she got. Kid's a mess."

Michael. They were talking about Michael. Who else could they be talking about? None of them—except Father Dominic—could see Jesse, or the RLS Angels. They could see only the two of us, Michael and me, both beaten, apparently, almost to death. Of course they assumed we'd done it to each other. Who else was there to blame?

Jesse. Reminded of him, my heart began to hammer in my broken chest. Where was Jesse? I lifted my head, looking around for him frantically in what had become a sea of uniformed police officers. Was Jesse all right?

Father Dominic misread my panic. He said, soothingly, "Michael's going to be all right. A severely bruised larynx, and some cuts and bruises. That's all."

"Hey." The EMT straightened. They were getting ready to load me into the ambulance. "Don't sell yourself short, kid." He was talking to me. "You got him real good. He won't be forgetting this little escapade for a long time to come, believe me."

"Not with all the time he's going to be spending behind bars for this," his partner said with a wink.

And sure enough, as they lifted me into the ambulance, I could see that Michael was sitting not, as I'd expected, in an ambulance of his own, but in the back of a squad car. His hands appeared to be cuffed behind his back. His throat may have been hurting him, but he was speaking. He was speaking rapidly and, if the expression on his face was any indication, urgently to a man in a suit I could only assume was a police detective of some kind. Occasionally, the man in the suit jotted something down on a clipboard in front of him.

"See?" The first EMT grinned down at me. "Singing like a canary. You're not going to have to worry about running into him in school on Monday. Not for a real long time."

Was Michael confessing? I wondered. And if so, what about? About the Angels? About what he'd done to the Rambler?

Or was he merely explaining to the detective what had happened to him? That he'd been attacked by some unseen, unmanageable force—the same force that had broken my ribs, split open my head, and busted my lip?

The detective didn't look as if anything Michael was telling him was all that extraordinary. But I happen to know from experience that this is the way detectives always look.

Just as they were closing the ambulance doors, Father Dominic cried, "Don't worry, Susannah. I'll tell your mother where to find you."

Can I just tell you that if this was supposed to comfort me, it totally didn't.

But right after that the morphine kicked in. And I found that, happily, I didn't care anymore.

CHAPTER 19

"This," Gina said, "is so not how I pictured spending my spring break."

"Hey." I looked up from the copy of *Cosmo* she'd brought me. "I said I was sorry. What more do you want?"

Gina seemed surprised by the vehemence in my tone.

"I'm not saying I haven't had *fun*," she said. "I'm just saying it's not how I pictured it."

"Oh, right." I tossed the magazine aside. "Yeah, it's been real fun, visiting me in the hospital."

I couldn't talk very fast with the stitches in my lip. Nor could I enunciate too well, either. I had no idea how I looked—my mother had instructed everyone, including the hospital staff, not to allow me access to mirrors, which of course led me to believe that I looked hideous; it had probably been a wise move, however, considering how I get when all I've got is a zit. Still, one thing for sure, I certainly *sounded* stupid.

"It's just for a few more hours," Gina said. "Until they get the results of your second MRI. If it comes out normal, you're free to go. And you and I can hit the beach again. And this time"—she glanced at the door to my private room to make sure it was all the way closed and no one could overhear her—"there won't be any pesky ghosts to ruin everything."

Well, that much was true, anyway. Michael's arrest, while anticlimactic, had nevertheless satisfied the Angels. They probably would have preferred to see him dead, but once Father Dominic convinced them of how miserable a sensitive boy like Michael was going to find the California penal system, they snapped right out of their murderous rage. They even asked Father Dominic to tell Jesse and me that they were sorry about the whole beating us into a bloody pulp thing.

I, for one, was not exactly ready to forgive them, even after Father D had assured me that the Angels had moved on to their afterlife destinations—whatever those might be—and would be troubling me no more.

Jesse's opinion on the matter I did not know. He had not deigned to grace either Father Dom or me with his presence since the night the Angels had attacked us. He was, I feared, extremely upset with me. Seeing as how the whole thing had been my fault, I didn't exactly blame him. Still, I wished he'd stop by, if only to yell at me some more. I missed him. More, I knew, than was probably healthy.

Damn that Madame Zara, anyway, for being right.

"You should hear what everyone at school is saying about you," Gina said. She was perched on the end of my hospital bed, already clad in her bikini, over which she'd thrown a leopard print baby doll dress. She wanted to waste as little time as possible when we finally got to the beach.

"Oh, yeah?" I tried to drag my thoughts from Jesse. It wasn't easy. "What are they saying?"

"Well, your friend Cee Cee's writing this story about you in the school paper...you know, the whole amateur sleuth angle of it all, how you caught on that it was Michael who'd committed all these heinous crimes and set out to trap him—"

"Something," I said drily, "that I'm sure she heard from you."

Gina looked innocent. "I don't know what you're talking about. Adam sent you those"—Gina pointed at an enormous bouquet of pink roses on the window sill—"and Mr. Walden, according to Jake, is taking up a collection to get you a complete set of Nancy Drew books. He apparently thinks you have a crime-solving fixation."

Mr. Walden was right about that. But my fixation wasn't on solving crimes.

"Oh, and your stepdad's thinking about buying a Mustang to replace the Rambler," Gina informed me.

I made a face, then regretted it. It was hard to make expressions of any kind with my sore lip, not to mention the stitches in my scalp.

"A Mustang?" I shook my head. "How are we all supposed to fit into a Mustang?"

"Not for you guys. For himself. He's giving you guys the Land Rover."

Well, that, at least, made sense.

"What about…" I wanted to ask her about Jesse. After all, she was sharing a room with him—alone, thanks to my being held overnight in the hospital for observation. The thing is, she didn't know it. About Jesse, I mean. I still hadn't told her about him.

And now, well, there didn't seem to be any reason to. Not now that he wasn't speaking to me anymore.

"What about Michael?" I asked instead. None of my other visitors—my mother and stepfather; Sleepy, Dopey, and Doc; Cee Cee and Adam; even Father Dom—would tell me anything about him. The doctors had advised them that the topic might be "too painful" for me to discuss.

As if. You want to know what's painful? I'll tell you what's painful. Having two broken ribs, and knowing that for weeks, you're going to have wear a one-piece to the beach in order to hide the black and blue marks.

"Michael?" Gina shrugged. "Well, you were right. What you said about him keeping stuff on his computer. The police got a warrant and confiscated his PC, and it was all there—journals, emails, the schematics of the Rambler's brake system. Plus they found the wrench he used. You know, on the bolts that held the guardrail in place? They matched the metal tracings. And the clippers he used to snip the Rambler's brake line. They got brake fluid off the blades. The boy didn't do such a good job cleaning up after himself, it appears."

I'll say.

He was arrested on four counts of first-degree

murder—the RLS Angels—and six counts of attempted murder: five for those of us who'd been in the Rambler the afternoon the brakes had given out, and one for what the police were convinced Michael had done to me out at the Point.

I didn't correct them. I mean, it wasn't like I was about to sit there and go, "Uh, yeah, about my injuries? Yeah, Michael didn't inflict them. No, the ghosts of his victims did that because I wouldn't let them kill him."

I figured it was just as well to let them go on thinking it was Michael who was responsible for my broken ribs and the fourteen stitches in my scalp... not to mention the two in my lip. I mean, after all, he'd been *going* to kill me. The Angels had just interrupted him. If you thought about it, they'd actually saved my life.

Yeah. So they could kill me themselves.

"So listen," Gina was saying. "Your grounding—you know, for sneaking out and getting into a car with Michael when your mother had told you expressly not to—isn't supposed to start until after I leave. I say we spend the next four days at the beach. I mean, there's no way you're going to school. Not with broken ribs. You wouldn't be able to sit down. But you can certainly *lie* down, you know, on a towel. I should be able to talk your mom into letting you do *that*, at least."

"Sounds good to me," I said.

"Ex," Gina said. She apparently meant excellent, only she'd shortened it—much in the way Sleepy often shortened words because he was too lazy to say all the syllables. Thus pizza became "'za," Gina became "G." She had, I realized, more in common with Sleepy than I'd ever guessed.

"I'm going to get a Diet Coke," she said, climbing down from my bed—careful not to jostle the mattress since the nurse had already come in twice and warned her not to. Like I hadn't consumed enough Tylenol with codeine to block out the pain. Somebody could have dropped a safe on my head and I probably wouldn't have felt it.

"You want?" Gina asked, pausing by the door.

"Sure," I said. "Just make sure—"

"Yeah, yeah," she said over her shoulder as the door swung slowly shut behind her. "I'll find a straw somewhere."

Alone in my room, I adjusted the pillows behind me carefully, and then sat there, staring at nothing. People who are on as many painkillers as I was tend to do that a lot.

But I wasn't thinking about nothing. I was thinking, actually, about what Father Dominic had told me when he'd visited a few hours ago. In what could only be the cruelest of ironies, the morning after Michael's arrest, his sister, Lila Meducci, had wakened from her coma.

Oh, it wasn't like she'd sat up and asked for a bowl of Cheerios, or anything. She was still severely messed up. According to Father D, it was going to take her months, even years, of rehabilitation to get her back to the way she'd been before the accident—if ever. It would be a long, long time before she'd be able to walk, talk, even eat on her own again like she used to.

But she was alive. She was alive and she was conscious. It wasn't much of a consolation prize for poor Mrs. Meducci, but it was something.

It was as I was reflecting over the vagaries of life that I heard a rustle. I turned my head just in time to catch Jesse trying to dematerialize.

"Oh, no, you don't," I said, sitting up—and jolting my ribs quite painfully, I'd like to add. "You come back here right now."

He came back, a sheepish expression on his face.

"I thought you were asleep," he said. "So I decided to come back later."

"Baloney," I said. "You saw I was *awake,* so you decided to come back later when you were sure I was asleep." I couldn't believe it. I couldn't believe what I'd caught him trying to do. This hurt, I discovered, way more than my ribs. "What, you're only going to visit me when I'm unconscious now? Is that it?"

"You've been through an ordeal," Jesse said. He looked more uncomfortable than I'd ever seen him. "Your mother—back at the house—I heard her tell everyone they weren't to do anything to upset you."

"Seeing *you* won't upset me," I said.

I was hurt. I really was. I mean, I'd known Jesse was mad at me for what I'd done—you know, that whole tricking-Michael-into-coming-out-to-the-Point-so-the-RLS-Angels-could-kill-him thing—but not even to want to *talk* to me anymore....

Well, that was harsh.

The hurt I felt must have shown in my face since when Jesse spoke, it was in the gentlest voice I'd ever heard him use.

"Susannah," he said. "I—"

"No," I interrupted him. "Let me go first. Jesse, I'm sorry. I'm sorry for that whole thing last night. It was all my fault. I can't believe I did it. And I'll never, ever forgive myself for dragging you into it."

"Susannah—"

"I am the worst mediator," I went on. Once I had the ball rolling, I found it was hard to stop it. "The worst one that ever lived. I should be thrown out of the mediator organization. Seriously. I can't believe I actually did something that stupid. And I wouldn't blame you if you never spoke to me again. Only—" I looked up at him, aware that there were tears in my eyes. Only this time, I wasn't ashamed to let him see them. "It's just that you've got to understand: he tried to kill my family. And I couldn't let him get away with that. Can you understand that?"

Jesse did something then that he'd never done before. I doubt he'll ever do it again, either.

And it happened so fast, I wasn't even sure afterward if it had really happened, or if, in my drugged-out state, I imagined it.

But I'm pretty sure he reached out and touched my cheek.

That's all. Sorry if I got your hopes up. He just touched my cheek, the only part of me, I imagine, that wasn't scraped, bruised, or broken.

But I didn't care. *He'd touched my cheek.* Grazed it, actually, with the backs of his fingers, not the tips. Then he dropped his hand.

"Yes, *querida,*" he said. "I understand."

My heart started beating so fast, I was certain he could hear it. Plus, I probably don't need to tell you, my ribs really, really ached. Each pulse seemed to send my heart slamming into them.

"And the only reason I got so angry was because I didn't want to see *this* happen to you."

On the word *this,* he gestured toward my face. I must, I realized, have looked pretty bad.

But I didn't care. He'd touched my cheek. His touch had been gentle, and, for a ghost, warm.

Am I pathetic, or what, that a simple gesture like that could make me so head-over-heels happy?

I said, idiotically, "I'll be all right. I won't even need any plastic surgery, they said."

As if a guy born in 1830 even knows what plastic surgery is. God, can I spoil a mood, or what?

Still, Jesse didn't exactly draw away. He stood there looking down at me like he wanted to say more. I was perfectly willing to let him, too. Especially if he called me *querida* again.

Only it turned out he didn't call me anything. Because at that moment Gina came bursting back into the room clutching two cans of soda in her hands.

"Guess what?" she said as Jesse shimmered, and then, with a smile to me, disappeared. "I ran into your mom in the hallway, and she said to tell you your second MRI came out normal, and you can start getting ready to go home. She's having all the paperwork done right now. Isn't that great?"

I grinned at her, even though doing so hurt my split lip.

"Great," I said.

Gina looked at me curiously. "What are you so happy about?" she wanted to know.

I continued to grin at her. "You just said I get to go home."

"Yeah, but you looked happy before I said that." Gina narrowed her eyes at me. "Suze. What gives? What's going on?"

"Oh," I said, still smiling. "Nothing."

ABOUT THE AUTHOR

JENNY CARROLL has lived in Indiana, California, and France, and has worked as an assistant dorm manager at a large urban university, an illustrator, and a writer of historical romance novels (under a pseudonym). In addition to *The Mediator,* she is the author of the series *1–800-Where-R-You* and, under the name of Meg Cabot, *The Princess Diaries,* now a major motion picture from Walt Disney Co. She currently resides in New York City with her husband and a one-eyed cat named Henrietta. Be sure to visit Jenny at her Web site, www.jennycarroll.com

ROCKPORT PUBLIC LIBRARY
3 4856 00039941 5